First edition published in 2025 by Rookscroft Publishing
rookscroft.com

ISBN 978-1-0684543-2-5

Written and illustrated by Jayne Siroshton.

Printed in India

Books by Jayne Siroshton

All Feathers and Hats

Circus of the Crescent Moon

Into the Wild Woods

Thank you Ben for making this book possible,
and to Darin Simmons and Matthew Greydanus,
the inspiration
for two of the finest feathered friends a
writer could have.

Into the Wild Woods

Written and Illustrated
by
Jayne Siroshton

Elsie's Caravan

Pahpowee's Camp

The Clearing

The Meadow

The Lodge

Old Bear's Cabin

Judge D.P. Bonneville's House

Harvest Moon Mountains

The Salish Sea

The Mole's

The Church

Rookscroft

The Harbour

The Obscura

Chapter One

The Library

"Where do all the bees go in the winter?" asked Robin one morning, and he cocked his little head to one side as he waited for a reply.

"Well, I'm not really sure," I said, "but we can go to the library and perhaps find a book that will tell us."

"Can we really?" he asked. "Go to the library, I mean. Is it far? Will I need to wrap up? It's been very cold today."

Quentin, who had been warming his toes by the fire, sighed deeply before turning to speak, "It's as far as the end of the hallway, Robin. Honestly, don't you remember? The room with all the books..."

"Oh, the book room! Yes, I like that one," Robin cried excitedly. "When can we go?"

"Yes, the book room," said Quentin. "And we can go now, but we will need to wrap up warmly. This house is as cold as a tomb."

"I can make a fire," I suggested, "and maybe bring along a pot of tea and some currant buns to toast."

"That sounds like a plan," replied Quentin. "Perhaps I can find a book on roses; I'd love to identify my house."

"Oh yes!" cried Robin excitedly. "Do you suppose we could find the exact species? And do you think the bees might all be there? They could be using the fallen petals as tents to keep the rain off."

Quentin sighed and rolled an eye, and I noticed the flicker of a smile at the corner of his beak.

"I'm going to make up the fire," I said. "You two stay here by the range; I'll be back in no time."

The library was cold, and in the light of a late winter morning, it felt dreary and sad. I stacked a little pyramid of kindling in the hearth, and once it was lit, I added bricks of shiny coal from the scuttle.

The dancing flames brought the room to life.

I returned to the kitchen, where my friends were chatting amiably, and put together a tray of treats for us to share. Then, together, we went to the library and settled in for a lazy afternoon.

After we had eaten, we sat beside the fire where the coals glowed red in the grate. Quentin, who had just polished off a substantial toasted teacake, stared sleepily into the flames.

"I feel it's possible that spring will never arrive," he said.

"Oh no, that can't happen," replied Robin earnestly. "Spring has to come, Quentin. It's printed on the calendar."

"I think technically it's almost here," I said, "though I admit, it doesn't really feel like it today."

"Well, it better hurry up," Quentin replied, rising from his cushion and shaking out his neck feathers. "The teacakes are delicious, but I'm getting a bit of a paunch, and the only cure for that is a jolly good walk."

He stretched out his yellow legs, then rose and went over to the bay window, where he inspected the dreary day with a round yellow eye. "What's the weather supposed to be like tomorrow?" he asked.

Robin, who was perched next to a large open book, turned and looked out at the grey clouds before considering his topknot. "It will be dry and possibly sunny," he answered confidently.

"Splendid! Sounds like a good day for an outing," Quentin said. "I suggest we set out in the morning after breakfast and circle the lawn."

"I don't know if leaving the house is a good idea, Quentin," stammered Robin, who was studying a page of the book. "I think, all things considered, we should stay inside... How far are we from the sea?"

"Not far. It's just down the hill," answered Quentin. "How long do you suggest we stay in?"

"Forever," replied Robin, his voice shaking slightly.

Quentin jumped down. "Whatever are you looking at?" he asked as he crossed the room and hopped up beside his friend. "Oh dear," he said as he looked at the page. "I do see what you mean, or I would if I thought they were real... Honestly, Robin, this is a book of fictitious creatures, talking animals and the like, and clearly, they don't exist."

Robin and the Sea Monsters

"Not even the giant sea porcupine with tusks?" asked Robin. "That one looks particularly savage."

"I'm sure I'm safe in saying he is not living around here," replied Quentin.

Robin, somewhat reassured, turned the page with his little beak, which took some effort. "And this one?' he asked in a fearful whisper.

I leaned towards them and saw that they were staring at an Elizabethan map with a sea monster, labelled as a whale, rising from a curling wave with its mouth agape.

"Oh, those. Yes, those. Well, those ones are real," replied Quentin with authority, "but don't fret. They stay far off in the deep, and neither of us would be caught dead out there."

"Are you sure they can't get up to the house?" Robin asked, glancing towards the window. "You did say that the sea was just down the hill."

"Now, don't be silly," replied Quentin. "How do you suppose they would manage that? Walk up? They don't have legs, Robin. Now, do calm down. Say, why don't we look at that box together? I don't know about you, but I'm intrigued to see what's inside."

The box he was referring to was on the mantelpiece

above the fire, and its decorative edge had caught Robin's eye.

"Can we really?" he asked, forgetting about the book entirely. "I would love to peek inside."

"If you promise to be careful," I teased, lifting it down and placing it on the table before them.

"Very nice marquetry," commented Quentin admiringly. "Mother of pearl inlay, Victorian, I believe, and if I am not mistaken, a writing slope."

"A writing slope?" asked Robin.

"Would you mind doing the honours, Jayne?" said Quentin.

I turned the little key in the lock and lifted the lid to reveal the lovely interior. The slope itself was covered in dark green felt, worn from use, and guided at the edges. To the front, a glass ink pot with a silver lid sat snugly next to a writing quill on a curved walnut tray.

"Oh, I do say, that's quite the setup," commented Quentin approvingly. "I could do with one like that myself. Do they make them in a smaller size?"

"I'm not sure," I replied, "but we can keep an eye out."

"Is that a little catch in the lid?" asked Robin, indicating with his wing.

I looked and saw it too. "I think it is," I replied. "Well spotted."

I lifted it with the tip of my nail, and the door popped open.

"It's a secret compartment!" whispered Quentin, leaning in.

Inside was a small stack of old papers, which I removed and under them lay an iron door key. On top was a letter dated the twenty-fourth of April 1889 that read:

Dear Fritzzle,

What a magnificent time we had visiting the charming lodge in the forest that you constructed in honour of your great friend Esser Der Eichel, whom I know you dearly miss. The food and beer you left for us were divine and in such copious quantities that we took many of them home! Emmeline is rationing me as my eyes are bigger than my rather substantial belly.

I am sending along a sketch I made while visiting and returning the map and key. What a great deal of work it must have been to cobblestone the path through the forest, but it helped tremendously. The only regret of our visit was that you could not join us, perhaps next summer? Give our love to Isolde.

Sincerely, your old friend,

Alberto Fagiano.

Under the letter was a pen and ink drawing of the prettiest little building tucked between tall trees.

"It looks so small," said Robin as he leaned in to take a closer look. "Can we visit soon?"

"I am inclined to say no," replied Quentin. "The forest is dangerous; it's no place for ground birds like us."

"But Quentin," replied Robin, "the letter was written by a pheasant. Don't you see his last name?"

"I swear, he speaks such nonsense at times," whispered Quentin, glancing over and rolling an eye.

I set the picture to one side; beneath it was a small map sketched in ink, showing Rookscroft with a line leading from the kitchen door through the wheat field to the gate, then left along the lane. It continued until it reached the Wild Woods, where a web of lines curved off into the great beyond. One of the paths was drawn in a bolder line indicating the way to the lodge, which was depicted as a small building set back behind a low stone wall not too far up the hill.

Robin examined it carefully. "We must go," he said suddenly. "Oh please, can we? It looks like such a short walk, and it can't be far; you did say, Quentin, that you wanted to work off your paunch, whatever that is."

"And just how do you know that it's not far?" asked Quentin.

"Well, it's such a little map," replied Robin.

"I think it would be fun to go," I said. "That is, when the weather gets a little better."

Robin hopped down, raced across the room and in the blink of an eye, he was standing on the windowsill. "Look," he cried, pointing with his wing, "it's a red sky, so tomorrow will be a fine day. Can we please take a picnic?"

I joined him and looked out over the darkening landscape. The sky above was stormy and grey, but out to sea, a slash of blazing rose hovered over the snow-capped mountains beyond the sea.

The Friends in the Library

"I thought you said that red skies were bad," said Quentin as he hopped up between us.

"That depends on when they occur," replied the little quail. "And look at my topknot, Quentin, it's as light as air!"

"Well, you've never been wrong about the weather before," I said. "It can't be that far. Judging by the map, I would say perhaps four miles at the most. I've been feeling cabin feverish lately, and I suggest we go."

"And your cure for cabin fever is a cabin?" asked Quentin archly. "Honestly, I think this whole idea is a grave mistake. I thought our first outing would be a jaunt over the lawn, to the hedge, and back, then a cup of tea."

"I can make us a nice cake and treats to take along," I suggested. "And you know, if we take some good food and blankets, we can even stay the night."

"Are you quite mad!" cried Quentin. "A night in the Wild Woods? Do you have any idea what you're suggesting?"

"We'll be fine," I assured him. "A nice walk on a sunny day, and once we're there, we can get a good fire going. It'll feel like home in no time. And of course, if anything feels amiss, we'll turn around and come straight home, I promise... Oh, come on, let's have a little adventure!"

Quentin eyed me sternly. "I suppose I can go if we stick together," he said, "but you must know that I am not exaggerating the dangers that lurk in those woods, even perhaps for you. I have it on good advice that there are wild bears, boars, and even wolves up there!"

"I promise to keep us safe," I said. "I'll bring the carpet bag with the shoulder strap, and you can ride in it if you like."

"Excuse me, Quentin, but bears and wolves don't live in the Wild Woods," said Robin. "They live in forests, and those are very far away over the sea, and they can't get here because of the leviathans of the deep. That's a fancy name for the sea monsters on the map."

Quentin shook his head. "It's getting dark," he said. "I think it may be time for supper."

"I think you're right," I agreed, and we returned to the kitchen together.

I fed the fire and baked potato bread with currants and a Madeira cake while my friends chatted about what they hoped to see on our adventure. After dinner, we headed to bed to get an early night, but I lay awake with Quentin's words of warning running through my mind. I looked down towards my feet, where my friends lay sleeping, and whispered a promise to keep them safe. Then, I finally drifted off into my dreams.

Chapter Two

The Lodge

The following morning I was awoken by a weak winter sun that shone through the crack in my bedroom curtains. Robin's prediction had been right. I slipped on my dressing gown and headed downstairs where I gathered provisions: cake, currant bread, a jar of plum jam, apples, hazelnuts, a tin of black tea and a bottle of port. I wrapped them up in a thick wool blanket and tucked the whole bundle securely into my rucksack along with some matches and an old oil lamp to light our way.

Quentin and Robin had taken to sleeping in late on these dark winter mornings, and it was a while before they stirred and even longer until we were finally ready to leave. It was half past two in the afternoon when I finally closed the door behind us and we headed up the hill together through the fields.

The sun shone soft and white in the misty sky.

"Just ahead is my home," said Quentin excitedly. "Robin, I can't wait to show it to you. Perhaps we will move out there together in the spring." But as we approached, we saw, to our dismay, that the winter storms had flattened the twisted branches almost to the ground and the doorway was quite gone.

"Oh dear," whispered Quentin sadly as he inspected the tangle of spiny branches. "I'm not sure what is what, or which way's which. There's barely anything left of it."

"Don't worry, Quentin," replied Robin cheerily. "It will grow back, that's what my mother always said."

"About your house?" asked Quentin. "I did not know you lived in a bush."

"No, about my brother's toe," replied Robin. "He lost it in an accident."

Quentin shook his head. "I think we should continue," he suggested dryly.

"Don't worry," I said. "Robin's right, it will grow back... The bush, I mean. I'm not so sure about the toe. As soon as the spring comes it will be as wild and beautiful as ever and a wonderful place to spend the summer. We should carry on if we want to make it to the lodge, the better part of the day is already behind us."

We slipped through the gate and onto the lane, turned left and followed it down the hill. The hedgerows grew thick and tall on either side and despite their lack of leafy cover, they were teeming with life. The tiny brown birds, looking for a late lunch of sloes and rosehips, peeped and chattered as they hopped from branch to branch.

"They sound so sweet!" I said.

"That's because you can't understand what they are saying," replied Quentin. "And believe me, it's better that way. Say, is there room in your bag for Robin and me? I smell foxes ahead."

I paused, lowered the carpet bag to the ground and opened it wide for them to climb in. There was movement on the path ahead and to my delight six little fox children tumbled out of the hedge and raced off down the lane laughing together.

"I love them!" I gasped in delight. "I don't think I've ever seen anything so sweet before."

Quentin, who was now safely in the bag, cast me a glance. "Please proceed with caution, Jayne," he advised, "and remember my family. I don't want us to follow in their footsteps, thank you."

"I'm sorry, you're right," I replied. "Foxes mean different things to different people, but I promise you're safe in there. Let me lift you up."

I hoisted the bag strap up over my shoulder and continued walking. We turned a wide corner, and the towering Wild Woods swung into view, majestic and unknowable. Down below, the path wound into the trees and just before, to the right, tucked back in the bank, was a little home and huddled by its pale blue door stood the fox kits. As we approached, the door opened and a beautiful fox in a lavender dress stepped out and sniffed the air, then beckoned them inside. She turned her head and regarded us with her sparkling rust eyes.

"She smells Robin and me," hissed Quentin from the bag. "Keep walking."

I waved as we passed and she nodded in reply, then slipped into the house and softly closed the door. Her home was built into the hedge bank with a neat thatched roof and a lovely leaded window that looked out onto the lane. Next to it hung a sign that read Dr Foxton Surgery hours 9 till 4, and as we passed I glanced inside and saw the doctor working at his desk.

Violet and Her Family

"Is it safe to come out now?" asked little Robin.

"Stay low," hissed Quentin, "until we are well past."

We continued along until we reached the stone gateposts that marked the entrance to the Wild Woods, and there I paused to look at the map. "See here," I said, angling the paper towards my friends, "this is where we are."

Scuffing the ground with the toe of my boot, I pushed the soft earth aside revealing a cobblestone. "Yes, look you can see the path, it's here on the map. Now we just need to follow it all the way up to the lodge."

"It looks dark in there," said Quentin dubiously, staring into the trees.

"Perhaps it's night already," suggested Robin.

I stepped forward, into the woods where the sky was obscured by the branches of trees and the air became muffled and still. Thickets of glossy ferns grew from the moss-covered rocks that lined the path. It was an unfamiliar, disconcerting place. There was no more chatter of birds, or playing foxes, even Quentin and Robin fell silent as we entered the fabled realm.

My feet sunk into soft pine needles as I made my way along the path. I was filled with peace, reverence and awe;

we had entered a vast green cathedral built by nature herself. We began to head uphill and my breathing became more laboured as I followed the twisting path that led up through the trees. A strange cry pierced the air as a large bird swooped low across the trail and landed on the side of a mossy trunk where it paused and watched us with its white-rimmed eye.

"Hello," I said. "You must be a pileated woodpecker, I'm Ja..." But before I could finish, it opened its pointed beak and let out an angry cry, then took to the air and looped off through the trees.

"They are not the same here," hissed Quentin. "We should turn back and go home while we still can."

"I just thought that... Well, wasn't Hieronymus a woodpecker, and he ran a circus?" I explained.

"They're different here," replied Quentin. "The woods and forests are filled with creatures who do not welcome us or our provincial life; they value the ancient ways."

"What about Bill?" I asked. "He came from hereabouts."

"He left," replied Quentin, "and I strongly suggest we do the same."

"Can we go just a little further, please?" begged Robin.

"There's a stream on the map with a bridge over it and I've never been on a bridge before."

I paused and took the map from my pocket. "Yes, you're right," I agreed, as I traced my finger along the line of water. "It's quite a long way up though, just by the waterfall and once you're there, you are almost at the lodge."

"Did you say waterfall?" asked Quentin, brightening. "Well, that changes everything! To think, there might even be a path behind it. I've read about those in books."

"Wouldn't that be amazing," I said. "Perhaps there is one, I'd love to see that too. Why don't we carry on at least for a little while, and see how far we get?"

They both agreed, so I resumed my steady walk up the wooded hillside and after some time, we came to a fork in the road where the map suggested we take the path to the left. With my friends' consent, I followed it up past a rocky bend where it levelled off.

"I think we must be going around the side of the mountain now," said Quentin nervously, as he looked out from the bag. "See how sharply the ground drops off just there?"

"It does," I replied, "and if you look through the trees to the right, it looks like the ground goes up very sh...."

"Do you hear that?" Quentin interrupted excitedly, and he turned his head to the side to listen.

"Yes!" cried Robin in a shrill high voice. "It's the sound of falling water!"

"And that's what's known as a waterfall," corrected Quentin. "Now hurry along, Miss, and mind your step or we'll fall right off the side, and I'd like to see it before I die."

Laughing, I quickened my pace and with each step, the low rumble grew louder.

"It's like walking up to a dragon!" cried little Robin, and he wasn't wrong, for the ground seemed to shake beneath my feet. We rounded a corner and stood before the thundering majesty of the falls. My words can't describe its power, and I stood in awe, hoping to see the top, but it was far above us, shrouded in clouds. The shining sheet of water plummeted from a great height, an immense white curtain that foamed and churned as it plunged into a dark pool before us.

The Falls

I stood in silent rapture, enfolded in the misty spray, until Quentin cocked his head toward me and shouted, "This is all very splendid, but my feathers are getting wet."

"You're right, I'm getting soaked through," I shouted back.

"I don't think it's just the waterfall," cried Robin. "If I'm not mistaken, there are also raindrops and I think even some ice."

Glancing down at my arm, I realised that he was right. A few ice-shining crystals flashed against the dark green wool of my coat sleeve.

The light was fading, and a soft mist rose from the water, escaping the bank. This was no time to get lost. I spotted the stone bridge we had seen on the map. It was to our left, between the trees, half covered in moss.

"We are almost there," I cried. "Just a little further, there's the bridge."

I made my way to it, away from the falls, and the air grew calmer as silence returned.

"If this state of this bridge is anything to go by, I don't hold out much hope for the lodge," said Quentin dubiously as we drew near.

"Can we walk across it?" Asked Robin excitedly "I've always dreamed of standing on a real bridge."

"I think we can manage that," I answered brightly. As we crossed over they leaned out and looked cautiously over the side at the dark stream that ran below.

The mist was drifting over the path, and I felt cold and tired as we turned the final bend, and suddenly, there it was! Behind a low stone wall. The little lodge sat proudly between the towering trees, and my heart leapt at its fairytale beauty.

"At least the roof seems intact," commented Quentin as we drew near. "Can you lower the bag, please, so we can stretch our legs?"

They both hopped out and hurried ahead of me to the front door.

"Do you have the key, Jayne?" asked Robin. "I can't wait to see inside."

The Lodge in the Wild Woods

I fumbled in my pocket and brought out the old iron key, then turned it in the lock, and with a little push, the old door creaked open.

The room was almost dark. I could just make out the fireplace made of smooth, rounded stones that rose up to meet the ceiling. Near to the hearth, an overstuffed sofa sat comfortably on an oriental rug. I laid my rucksack down, untied the oil lamp, and set it on a side table. My fingers felt cold and numb, as I fumbled with the matches before lighting the wick. As the flame grew stronger, the room lit up in a friendly glow, and I began to look around. On the far side of the fireplace, was a rustic staircase, and underneath a panelled alcove that housed a single bed. Over on the far wall, the room extended back to form a small kitchen with a black iron range and a simple sink, and in the corner was a door with a stained-glass window which I assumed led to a bathroom.

"This really is lovely," I said to my friends, who stood on the sofa assessing the room.

"Oh, look!" cried Robin. "There's a bookshelf, what a treat!" and he hastened over to take a closer look.

I noticed that the gap between the bookshelves and fireplace was stacked with firewood. "I'll get it nice and cosy for us," I said, and I took the kindling from my bag and began to make a fire.

"Oh, they do have some classics," commented Quentin (he had joined Robin and was inspecting the books). "Beau Geste, Tarzan and the Lost Empire, Stories from China... Do you know that my family was originally from the Orient?"

"Were they really?" exclaimed Robin. "And where is that?"

"If I find a map, I can show you," replied Quentin. "But please don't ask too much of me this evening, the walk has quite wiped me out. Now, how about this little treasure..."

While they chatted, I looked through the cupboards where I found some old plates and glasses that seemed surprisingly clean. After a quick rinse in the sink, I laid them on the low table by the fireside and started to unpack the food. As I brought out the fruit cake, I was amused to see that all the candied cherries had been picked out of the wax paper wrapping via a small hole.

"Oh, that would be me," admitted Quentin when he saw me looking it over. "I needed sustenance to keep going."

"Would you like me to help with the books?" I offered, and without waiting for their reply, I scooped up a good dozen of them and brought them to the sofa. "This will give us something to do 'til bedtime," I said. "Hop up, there's plenty to eat. Would either of you care for a little Port? It's very warming."

I laid the wool blanket out over the cushions and was joined by my friends. We ate and drank and thoroughly entertained ourselves while the logs spat and sizzled in the hearth and the rain drummed on the slate roof above. We looked through an old catalogue together, where, much to Quentin's delight, we saw a picture of a large ginger jar featuring golden pheasants in a field. Robin found a book titled "The Waterways of the Amazon" which delighted and terrified him in equal measure, and soon the worries of the day began to slip from our minds, and the room felt quite like home.

The evening continued peacefully until Quentin (who was explaining the origins of fine porcelain) happened to glance up over the fireplace and let out a terrible scream. My friends stared up in horror, and there, in the gloom, a huge boar's head hung from the wall, his ivory tusks glinting in the flickering firelight.

"Wwwww... we have to leave before it sees us," stammered Quentin. "That thing is a monster!"

"It's from the Book of Beasts!" cried Robin, staring wide-eyed. "But I thought you told me they weren't real!"

They were under the blanket in a flash.

"Don't worry," I soothed, trying to suppress a giggle. "That's the head of a wild boar. It's very old, and I wouldn't be surprised if he hasn't been hanging there since this lodge was built. I know that Fritzzle loved boars, and for all we know, he might have been a pet."

"Then he's the beast!" cried Quentin. "Who would do such a thing to a friend?"

"Those Victorians were a little different," I replied. "I agree it seems macabre to us, but I believe they thought of things differently back then-wearing necklaces with the hair of the departed, that kind of thing. Now settle down, he won't hurt you; he has been dead for a century at least."

"Could he have been a truffle pig?" asked Quentin, peeking out. "I have always fancied trying one-a truffle, that is-and I believe they grow in forests just beneath the surface of the soil around trees."

"There's a good chance he hunted for them," I replied, "either for himself or to share."

"Perhaps we can find some on our way home?" suggested Robin excitedly. "What are they again?"

"Truffles," replied Quentin, "and before you ask, not the chocolate kind. These are in the mushroom family, and I hear they are delicious. Oh, what I wouldn't give to be back in the kitchen with a nice truffle-infused soup."

"Well, we can certainly look on the way home," I said. "I've read they grow very close to the surface, just under the pine needles. We might even find some if we scratch about."

"Really? How exciting!" cried Robin. "That means when we wake up, we will be hunting for treasure!"

I smiled at them both, and my eyes drifted across the room to the large silver horn of a gramophone player, on top of the bookcase.

"Oh, look," I said, pointing over. "I think we can have music, if I can find a record."

"A record?" Robin asked. "Is that one of those thin books on the shelf?"

He was right. On the shelf below the gramophone lay a little stack of records in their old, yellowing paper. I crossed the room to take a closer look. Each one had such pretty lettering, and they were all intriguing, but one in particular caught my eye.

"I've found just the one," I told my friends. "Now let's see if I can get it to work."

I wound the handle, lifted the lid and placed the fragile

record carefully on the turntable, then switched the lever, which set it spinning. I felt a little nervous as I carefully lowered the arm, but thankfully the needle slipped easily into the groove. There was a moment of soft static before the music began-scratchy and joyful-and after the first refrain, a man began to sing in a playful, happy voice.

The birds craned to hear the words, their heads angled to the side, and after the end of the verse, the chorus began: "When the red, red robin..."

Robin instantly leapt into the air. "He's singing about me!" he cried.

"...bob, bob, bobbin' along..." sang the man.

Robin's eyes were round with excitement, and to our delight and amazement, he began to dance, hopping first forward and then backward to the music like a little mechanical toy.

I caught Quentin's eye, which sparkled with amusement as we watched.

"Well, just look at you go!" encouraged Quentin, with laughter in his voice.

"I'm good, aren't I!" cried Robin. "I never knew someone wrote this song just for me."

He continued to dance, hopping all about the room, and I clasped my hands to my mouth to stop myself from laughing at the strange and charming sight.

When the song ended with a hiss and scratch, and the arm had returned to its original position, Robin stood quite still.

"Again, again!" he cried. "And this time, please join me, Quentin! It's so much fun, and I would love us to dance together."

"Oh, go on," I chided. "How often do you get the opportunity?"

"I suppose I might as well," replied Quentin. "But this performance will be kept between us, and I expect good compensation in the form of a nice dinner when we get home. Now, no laughing... I'll be watching."

"Don't worry, Quentin," replied Robin. "I'm going to find truffles for you, and we will have a feast fit for a king!"

"If we are to dance, I'll lead," said Quentin, getting to his feet. "And none of this flitting around the room-we'll stay on the carpet by the fire. Four steps forward, four steps back, starting with your right foot when I say..."

"And which would that be?" asked Robin, looking

down.

"The one nearest the grate," replied Quentin. "I believe we are as ready as we will ever be..."

I returned to the gramophone and started the record, which hissed softly for a moment before the music began.

Now, I have promised faithfully not to go into details of the dance that ensued, but I made no promise that I would not draw a little picture of the event, so here it is.

My friends danced until they could barely stand, as I watched admiringly. What a beautiful evening we spent together there by the crackling fire. It was very late when we made a bed up on the sofa and snuggled down for a good night's sleep.

"Well, I must say, this has been a hoot," whispered Quentin, "and tomorrow we have home and good food to look forward to."

"Yes, treasure hunting and truffles," replied Robin, yawning. "What a day it will be! I've never been so happy." And with that, we fell asleep.

Quentin and Robin Dancing

Chapter Three
Auntie Winnie

I try not to think about the following morning.

It was almost dark when I first woke up, and I wasn't sure where I was. It took a moment for my mind to recall the events of the previous day and remember the lodge. I looked around and recognised the dimly lit room, I saw the embers glowed under the ash and my friends slept soundly at my feet. Quentin's long tail was wrapped around them both, and Robin's little head rested on a cushion by his cheek. I noticed that they breathed together as they slept and smiled to myself before drifting back to my dreams.

Sometime later, I was woken by a cold breeze. It was morning now, and I could see the room quite clearly. The window by the front door was slightly ajar. I slipped out of bed and went over to close it, looking out onto the dull, misty forest before taking the latch and pulling it shut.

I decided we should set out early, so I stoked the embers, fed the fire, put a pot on to boil water for tea, and toasted a slice of currant bread on a flat iron pan. The smell of cooking and the spit of the logs woke Quentin.

"Well hello," he called over in his croaky morning voice. "What are you up to over there?"

"Just making breakfast before we go home," I replied as he stretched out his legs and sat up on the sofa. "Did you sleep well?"

"As well as can be expected in a cabin in the woods," replied Quentin. "It's been an adventure, I'll admit, but I am excited for us to head back today. Do you suppose we will be there by lunchtime?"

"If we crack on, I don't see why not," I said. "Let's eat a good breakfast and be on our way. We can search for truffles as we walk back down the trail and still be back in time to settle in before evening."

"Sounds like a plan!" exclaimed Quentin happily. "I'll wake Robin."

"Why don't we let him sleep a little longer," I suggested. "He wore himself out with all that dancing; his legs are so small, and you know how excited he is about the truffle hunt; it will be hard to keep him in the bag."

"You're right," agreed Quentin, settling back down. "Did you bring preserves for the toast? It feels like a plum kind of morning."

"Then you are in luck," I replied, fishing the jar from the bottom of my rucksack. "Would you like me to help you with the application?"

"I would expect nothing less," answered Quentin. "We don't want my feathers getting sticky, do we?"

I laid out a plate for him and a saucer of tea, and we ate in silence beside the fire. When we were finished, I busied myself collecting our belongings and tidying the room while Quentin went over to wake up Robin.

A moment later, he let out a scream. "He's gone, oh no, he's gone!" he cried.

I turned and saw my dear friend's face; his eyes were round with panic. "Oh Jayne, he is gone; one of those night creatures has taken him!"

"That can't be so," I replied as I made my way over to him. "This morning when I first woke up, he was sleeping next to you, up by your chin."

"Well, he isn't there now," cried Quentin, scratching wildly at the blanket with his feet. "Help me, please help me find him!"

I lifted the blanket from the sofa and carefully shook it out, then lifted the cushions and ran my hands gingerly around the edges, but he was nowhere to be found.

I was aware of my heart thumping in my chest.

"Robin!" cried Quentin, his voice almost breaking. "Oh Robin, do come out! Please, please come out."

And then I remembered the window and went over to check it again. I lifted the latch, and it opened into the cold morning air.

"What are you doing?" asked Quentin urgently.

"Well, this morning, when I woke for the second time, this window was open," I replied as calmly as I could. "Perhaps he popped out to get a little air."

"Get some air?" cried Quentin. "Why, there's plenty of that in here! Quick, open the door; he might be waiting on the step!"

I turned the key and pulled the door open. Outside, it was silent and grey. Quentin stepped out in front of me; he stood on his toes, neck stretched, head tipped back, and let out a loud, eerie cry. He suddenly looked so out of place, a fantastical bird who belonged on a gilded china plate, not some muddy forest trail.

The woods were silent.

"Come along in, Quentin," I suggested with urgency. "We'll find him; he can't have gone far."

We were about to go back inside when I noticed them below the window; a line of tiny footprints that ran along the edge of a puddle.

"Look," I gestured to Quentin, "I think they're Robin's."

Quentin bent down and inspected them closely. "You're right, let's go!" he cried.

I ran back inside, pulled on my boots, snatched my coat and bag from the hook, and shut the door behind me as I left. We followed the broken line of footprints to the gate. Quentin spotted them leading left, and we retraced our route from the day before and headed back towards the falls. Robin's little prints wove from one side of the lane to the other, sometimes looping back on themselves.

"Whatever was he doing?" asked Quentin, shaking his head.

"I'm not sure. It almost seems as though he was

looking for something."

"You don't suppose it was truffles?" Quentin asked, and it suddenly all made sense, for here and there, tiny patches of pine needles had been scratched away by his dear little feet.

"You're right," I said excitedly. "He can't have gone far."

"Silly bird, he's quite mad," sighed Quentin. "Why, he's no bigger than a decent-sized truffle himself. How was he thinking he was going to collect them?"

"He's never actually seen one, so he probably has no idea how large they can be," I replied. "And to be fair, he doesn't have a great understanding of scale."

"You're right there," sighed Quentin. "Well, I can promise you this, when we find him, which I feel could be at any moment, I'll never let him out of my sight again. He seems to be lacking any sense of self-protection. He's practically a walking hors d'oeuvre."

I keenly remember the feeling of hope as we followed his trail along the path, for I was certain he was close by and that at any moment, he would pop out next to us, and we could go home together. Quentin spotted his little prints between the grasses to the right of the bridge, and we carefully followed them down to the riverbank. It was there, next to the swift, dark stream, that they abruptly ended.

It took a moment to realise the implications of our discovery, and we stood together staring down at the last impression his little toes had made in the dark mud by the water's edge.

"Oh no," whispered Quentin in disbelief. "He can't swim; I know he can't swim."

He looked up at me, shaking, his eyes wide with fear.

"It's going to be OK," I said, and crouching beside him, I laid my hand on the soft feathers of his back.

"How can you possibly know that?" he asked, staring. "How can you possibly know?"

I couldn't answer at first. I looked around at the towering trees; if it wasn't for the path, we would be lost ourselves. "I feel it," I finally said, though that was a lie. "We'll find him. Hop in the bag and wait here while I run back to the lodge. I'm going to leave the window open in case he returns before we do."

Quentin did as I suggested, and I was soon back at the little house, I cracked open the window, threw some logs on the fire, and left a slice of Madeira cake next to a scribbled note that read, "Dear little Robin, We are out looking for you. Stay here. We'll be back soon. Love Quentin and Jayne."

As I returned along the path, I saw Robin's footsteps again, and my eyes filled with tears because, in truth, I believed we had lost him. But when I approached the stream and saw poor Quentin sitting anxiously in the bag, I pulled myself together and put on a brave face.

He turned. "Any sign?" he asked hopefully.

"Not yet," I replied, "but why don't I tuck the blanket around your back, and you can ride along for a bit. I think we should follow the stream along; if he did slip in, he might very well have managed to climb out a little further on."

I hoisted the strap onto my shoulder and began our slow walk along the bank. It was a difficult journey; the ground was muddy and overgrown with thick grass and brambles whose spiny tendrils crossed the trail and hung down into the murky water. Inch by inch, we examined the ground for any clue; we saw the wide footprints of a river otter and the long fingers of a heron as it perched looking for a meal, the cloven hooves of a solitary deer, and the handprints of a raccoon. There were plenty of signs of every kind of forest creature, but not a single print created by the delicate foot of a lesser-spotted dip quail named Robin, not one.

"What was that?" asked Quentin urgently. "I think I heard my name."

"You did?" I replied, and we both fell silent, listening intently, but the only sound was the soft babbling of water as the stream ran by.

"Robin, is that you?" called Quentin, and we listened again, but no answer came.

"Let's keep going," he finally said. "My mind must be tricking my ears."

We continued along to where the stream became wide and shallow, and fish darted about in the clear, cold water over the smooth stones of the river bottom. Up ahead, I saw a crude bridge fashioned from fallen logs.

"Why don't we cross over?" I suggested, and Quentin sadly nodded in reply.

The bridge was made from three large logs laid neatly side by side. To the left, the stream we had travelled was joined by another that wove towards us from between the trees. They merged at the bridge, running under it together, and spilled into a woodland pond ringed with trees. At the water's edge was a small dwelling, low and wide. It was made of logs with a curved turf roof. A ribbon of wood smoke rose from its stone chimney and curled into the misty sky.

"Look, Quentin," I whispered, pointing, "look over there. Someone's home, and maybe they can help."

Quentin slowly raised his head and gazed blankly out across the pond. "Beware," he cautioned, "this IS the Wild Woods, and goodness knows what creature lurks behind that door. But if Robin is truly gone, then perhaps it's my time to go too, so carry on, Miss, and do as you please."

I crossed the bridge and followed a narrow, well-worn path along the water's edge that led me to the little home. The curved front door barely came up to my waist and was almost as wide as it was high. The welcoming glow of an oil lamp shone from a round window by the side of it.

"I don't like the look of this," hissed Quentin nervously.

"Why don't you tuck down until we see who's here," I suggested, and his head retracted slowly as I began to knock on the wide plank door.

At first, no one answered, so I knocked again, this time a little louder, and moments later, I heard faint footsteps and a soft dragging sound.

Aunty Winnie

"Hold on, hold on, I'll be there in a minute," said a sweet, muffled voice. "Now, where did I put the...Ah yes, there it is..." and the door slowly opened.

Before us stood a stout beaver with twinkling eyes. She wore a green dress that grazed the floor and several shawls layered one over the other, secured with a large amber pin. "Oh, there you are!" she said warmly as though she had been expecting us all day. "You look cold, dearie, come on in. You'll catch your death on a day like this, you will... Come in, come in! Don't be shy, and mind the step." With this, she turned and made her way back into the house.

I crouched down as I passed through the little entrance, but once inside, the ceiling was high enough for me to stand.

"Now you're a tall one, aren't you," said the beaver admiringly. "You must have eaten all your carrots and plenty of willow sticks to grow as big as that. Now, come over and get by the fire. Hurry now, dear, and don't be shy."

I crossed the room; her furniture looked very comfortable but much too small for me, so I sat on the floor next to the hearth.

"Well, let me see," said the beaver, making her way over and examining me closely. "Now you're down at my height; let me get a good look at you. Don't mind me; my eyes aren't what they once were." She peered closely at my face as though looking at a painting. "Yes," she mumbled as though answering a silent question, "Yes, kind eyes, yes... I'm your Aunty Winnie, dear. Would you like some tea?"

Before I could answer, she was over by the stove, putting dried leaves into a wooden cup and ladling on hot water. Once done, she shuffled back and handed the drink to me before making a cup for herself; then, she sat on the opposite side of the fireplace and picked up her knitting. "Don't mind me, dear," she said. "My mind likes to keep my fingers busy. Now, what's your name?"

"My name is Jayne," I replied, "and thank you for the tea."

"My pleasure, dear," she said, smiling warmly and nodding her head.

I watched as she paused to inspect the stitches, then settled down and began to knit rapidly. "Now, what brings you here?" she asked, looking at me directly. "It's a long way out on a day like this."

"We came yesterday, my friends and I, to spend the night in a little lodge near the waterfall, but when we woke up this morning, one of my friends was missing."

A flash of worry crossed Winnie's face. "Lost, oh yes, that happens, dear, but you will find your friend, I'm sure. But it's no use looking when you're cold, dear, no use at all. Cold numbs the mind, you see, so get nice and warm by the fire and drink up... Now, where did you last see your friend, dear? Do tell."

I felt a movement in the bag by my side and half expected to see Quentin poke out his head, but he kept low and out of sight.

"Well, early this morning," I replied, "his tracks led down to the stream and then stopped; I think he might have fallen in."

"Oh, that's no good," replied Winnie, "unless your friend is a fish, that is..."

"No, he's no fish," I replied sadly. "He's a little bird, a very little bird."

"Is he a duck?" asked Winnie hopefully. "I know they can swim, or a goose perhaps?"

"He's neither," I answered, "just a very small quail, very small indeed."

"A quail in the woods," said Aunty Winnie. "Why, I've never seen one of those before."

"That's because he doesn't belong in the woods!" cried Quentin, as he popped into view. "We should never have come, never have come!"

"Oh gracious me," gasped Winnie, flinging her arms into the air. "Well, look at that, we have another visitor. Would you like some tea, too?"

"We don't have time for tea," snapped Quentin, his heart racing. "Our friend is missing; he is very small, lost, and gone in all these trees. We don't have time for all this sitting and chatting. We have to go and find him now!"

"Not without tea, dear," replied Winnie calmly. "No, that would never do. It's cold out there, and as I was saying to Jayne, you need to warm your belly on a crisp day like this. Try a little of the brewed birch bark; it will help keep your mind sharp for looking."

Without waiting for an answer, she bustled over to the stove and poured a saucer of amber tea into a shallow bowl.

"Go ahead, dear, it's not too hot," she said kindly as she placed the drink on the floor next to the bag. Quentin leaned forward, and took a sip of tea.

"Interesting, it tastes very fresh," he commented once he was done.

"That's right, dear, now drink up. That tea will perk you up, it will." Winnie sat down in her chair and picked up her knitting.

"What are you making?" I asked.

"Well," replied Winnie, holding up the item and turning it in her hands, "it's a little sweater. See, now here are the arms." She held out two long, thin sleeves. "And I'm working on the neck." She lifted it by the needles, and I tried not to laugh, for the neck looked like another sleeve. "Oh dear," muttered Winnie, realising her mistake, "I seem to have got a bit lost somehow... But it has lovely big pockets, and pockets are always a blessing."

She lowered the sweater and continued knitting, adding more rows to the neck. "Now, back to your friend, dear, I don't suppose he had a boat with him? Boats can be handy when you fall in the water."

"I'm afraid not," I replied.

"Mmm, well, if he floated down this far, he'll be in the pond," she said. "The far end has always been dammed up; I patch it every spring, I do. Have you finished your tea, dear? When you're done, you can have a walk down there and see."

"Really, the pond, you say," said Quentin hopefully. "There's no time to lose, so let's be going." He slurped down the last sip and glanced anxiously around. "Right now would be a good time. Thank you for the drink."

Winnie studied him carefully. "Now here, young man," she said, "I believe I have something for you. Just a couple more rows, and I can cast off. Now onto the sofa so I can help you get it on."

Quentin shot me a puzzled glance.

Winnie knitted for a moment more and gnawed the sweater free, and before he had time to protest, she had the garment over his head.

"Get this off, I can't breathe!" he cried, or words to that effect.

"Nonsense, dear, stop complaining," Winnie responded. "Now, when I pull down, you push up your head."

I tried not to laugh as the long neck sleeve began to move and fill as Quentin slowly snaked his head through the tight tube.

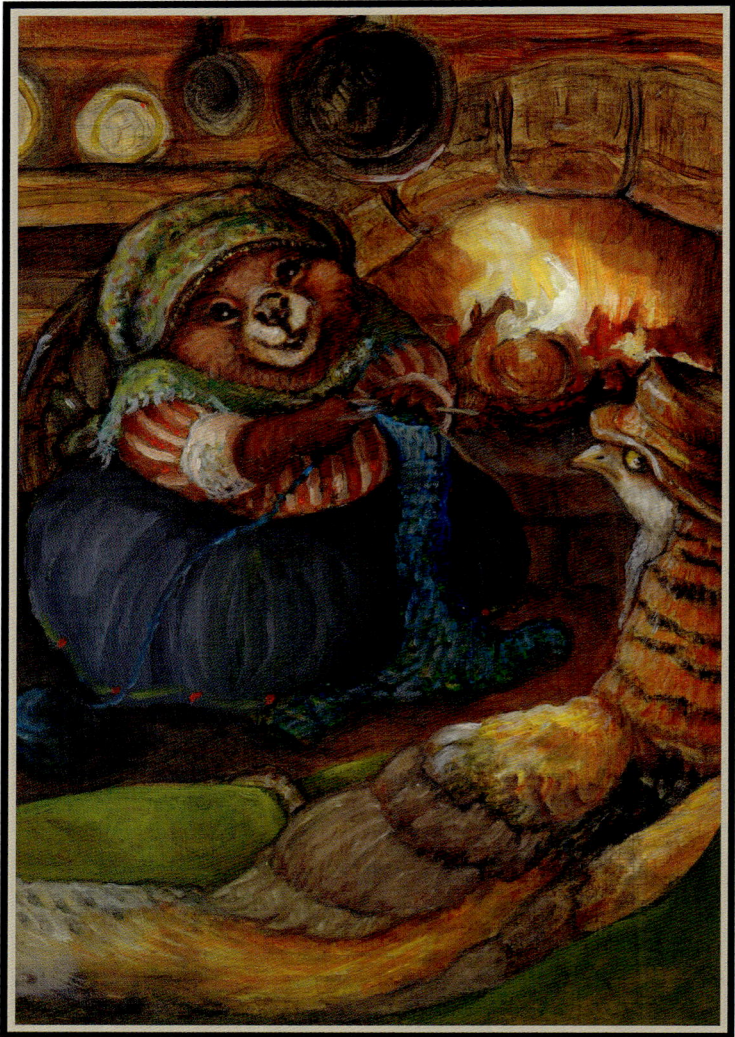

Winnie and Quentin

"I can't breathe," came his muffled cry.

"Nonsense, dear, you're almost there. You'll thank me when we're through, just one more push, beak up now, we're almost there, and..."

Quentin's head popped out, and he looked around indignantly as I tried to keep my composure.

"Well, now I know how being born feels... and all I can say is thank goodness for eggs," he said. "How do I look?"

"Don't fuss," scolded Winnie. "Stay still; I need to sort out what to do about these," and she pulled the body of the sweater down as far as it would go, then took the thin sleeves and held them out. "Oh yes, of course, silly me, that's how they go!" She brought them to the front and tied them in a bow. "Now that's very nice, dear, very nice indeed," she said proudly. "This will keep your lovely long neck warm, and that's important on a cold day like this."

"Thank you, but we really ought to be going," said Quentin. "We must find Robin before it's dark, and then we can all go home together and pretend this never happened."

"Yes," I agreed. "We really do need to be going, Winnie. Thank you, you've been so kind."

"The air really is very chilly today," said Winnie as she

stepped outside the door. "I could knit you a quick beak warmer if you'd fancy it?"

"Thank you for the invitation, but you've been generous enough already," Quentin replied.

"Well, before you go, I'll ask my friend if she has seen him," Winnie said, and she shuffled over to the edge of the pond and beckoned us over. "I'm sure she'd love to meet you. She enjoys company as much as I do."

Leaning over the dark water's surface, she began to wave.

"Hello down there!"

"Oh, hello to you too..." she replied to herself in a funny little voice.

"How have you been keeping?"

"Fine, thank you, and yourself?"

"Oh, not bad, not bad at all. I've got visitors today. They are missing their companion, a little bird named Robin. Have you seen him down there?"

"In the water, no. Did you suggest they look by the dam?"

"I did. They are just about to head over."

"Well, wish them well. I must say that the pheasant is wearing a lovely pullover."

"Why, thank you, I knitted it myself."

"Well, you did a lovely job."

I glanced at Quentin, who looked back in utter confusion.

"Have a nice day, dearie."

"You too, goodbye."

Winnie slowly straightened, pressing her brown hands on the small of her back as she eased herself up.

"She wishes you all the best, and he's not down there, thank goodness. Now you two go and have a good look around. Stop by before you leave. I'll keep the kettle on." And with these words, she turned and headed back towards her house.

"Well, that was more than a little odd," said Quentin once the door had closed behind her. "Living alone out here really takes a toll."

"I agree," I replied, "but she did seem very nice, and

she made you such a lovely scarf thingy."

"The less said about that, the better," replied Quentin. "You must promise never to paint me in it, and you'll need to help me cut it off before anyone sees it. Some things can never be lived down."

"The next time I find a pair of sharp scissors, I'll be happy to oblige, but at least it will keep you warm for now," I said.

We began our slow walk around the pond's muddy edge, searching for the slightest clue, but alas, there were none.

As we approached the dam, I saw that, like the bridge, it was constructed of logs laid tightly together. Winnie's handprints were in the dry mud, where she had worked to patch the holes, and I wondered if she had made it all herself.

A tiny bird popped out its head from between the logs; Quentin saw it too. "Robin is...!" he began, but before he could finish, it took to the air and flew off into the dark forest.

"Will we ever see him again?" asked Quentin feebly.

"Of course," I lied. "We mustn't give up hope. He's probably on one of his adventures without the slightest worry in his head. Let's look more closely; Winnie said the dam is our best bet to find him."

We slowly picked our way across the logs. It was a treacherous walk, with cold, dark water on either side. When we reached the middle, we paused and looked back along the length of the pond. To the right sat Winnie's house tucked into the bank, and on the far side, I could make out the bridge that led to the path back to the waterfall.

I cupped my hands around my mouth and repeatedly called, "Robin, oh Robin," in a sing-song voice.

Quentin joined in; his scratchy voice had an urgent tone, and our voices melted into the damp, dreary fog, but still, there was no reply. Below us, the dark body of a giant fish swam silently by. As it slipped into the depths, my heart rose in my throat.

"Do you suppose he...?" began Quentin as though reading my thoughts.

"Don't even think it," I said. "We can't."

Someone was watching; I looked ahead to where a heron stood, peering into the water.

"I think they eat small birds," hissed Quentin. And as he spoke, its head darted forward, and plunged silently into the water, returning moments later with a wriggling fish in its beak. I heard Quentin gasp as it tossed back its head, the fish slithered down its long neck and was gone.

"Gruesome," hissed Quentin. "You don't think?"

"No, I don't," I reassured him again. "Robin's too quick for a fate like that; remember how he moved last night when the music came on? That little bird has some fancy footwork. A heron wouldn't stand a chance."

Quentin laughed weakly. "Oh, he loved that song," he said. "I would give my egg tooth to be back there now when our only concern was how much cake was left. I wish with all my heart that we had never come here."

"Me too," I said. "I'm sorry I didn't listen to you in the library. Let's find him and go home. I've had my fill of this place. Let's keep going; we can pop in and say goodbye to Winnie before we leave."

Quentin dropped his gaze to the mud, and we slowly picked our way over the dam, inspecting every print until we reached the path on the other side.

"I don't think he's here," I said as we climbed off the logs and back onto the path, "but we ought to keep looking."

We continued around to where the reeds grew thick.

There was a movement ahead, and my heart skipped a beat.

"Robin," Quentin called out. "Is that you? Come along, do come out. It's time to go home."

Silence, then we heard it again, a soft rustle of feathers.

"Is that you, Robin?" I whispered hopefully. "Oh, I pray it's you, my little friend."

In my mind's eye, I saw him nestled in a bed of reeds, taking a quick nap; that's why he didn't answer. I stepped off the path toward the sound, and my foot sank ankle-deep into the boggy ground. Carefully, I parted the reeds and peered in; my mind had raced ahead... I would wrap him in my scarf and tuck him safely into my pocket. He would be chilled but fine, and we would return to the lodge to get warm by the fire. We would eat together and rest, and tomorrow, we would return home...

Reaching a little farther, I drew back more stalks, and there, straddled between the reeds, stood a tiny brown bird who stared at me indignantly before fluttering off in a flurry of tiny whistles.

"There is no need for that!" cried Quentin. "We have lost our friend, you fool; we are looking for our friend!" and he began to weep.

I pulled my foot from the mud, sat with him on the path, and both of us cried together.

A little while later, when the hot tears had dried on our cheeks, we sat in silent peace, listening to the wind in the trees. I saw beauty in the dark forest that reached toward the sky, reflected in the deep, still water of the pond. On the far side, a welcoming light shone from the window of Winnie's home, and as I watched, the door opened, and she stepped out, drawing the shawl around her shoulders as she waited for our return.

"Shall we carry on?" I asked.

"Yes," Quentin replied weakly. "Yes, let's."

"Would you like me to carry you, my friend?" I asked.

"I wouldn't say no," he answered. I scooped him into my arms, and we continued until we came to the wooden bridge we had crossed hours before.

"Maybe we should just go back to the lodge," suggested Quentin. "He might be there, waiting for us. That window you left open by the door is very low; why, it wouldn't take a moment for him to flutter back inside."

"Wouldn't that be perfect," I replied. "You're right; we should get back, but first, let's say goodbye to Winnie; she's waiting for us."

"Let's keep it brief," suggested Quentin. "If he's alone in the lodge, who knows what kind of mischief he'll get into."

We crossed back over and retraced our path towards Winnie's house.

"Saw you both on the far side, I did," she exclaimed as we drew near. "I hoped you would be heading back, so I put some soup on. It's slick on that path; I'm glad you didn't take a tumble. Now, step on lively, and we'll get you fettled up."

She opened the door wide, and the cosy interior beckoned.

"I'm sorry, but we don't have time," protested Quentin. "We have to head back to the lodge; I think he might be there."

"Oh, wouldn't that be a treat," replied Winnie. "But have some soup first. It's almost done."

We followed her in and took our places by the fire while Winnie fetched bowls from the dresser and placed a round of hard bread in each one. "They'll need a little broth to soften them up, but it will be nice and filling," she explained as she ladled the soup from an iron pot that hung above the flames.

"Here you go, dears," she said, handing a bowl to me and placing a second one in front of Quentin. "You might want to give it a minute to cool. Now I've been thinking, and I know someone who might be able to help you."

"Thank you, but I'm almost sure he's waiting for us at the lodge," said Quentin. "It would have been easy for him to double back there."

"I hope you're right, dear, but just in case, I'll give you instructions on how to find your way up to Elsie's."

"Is Elsie the friend who can help us?" I asked.

"Yes, she is, dearie. Now I've been thinking it over, and I have a plan."

She paused to pick over a basket of wool by her side and, after a moment, lifted something brown and narrow into the air by its needles and began to knit.

"Now, when you leave, follow the path along the stream, which will take you back to the lodge. I'm hoping that your friend has found his way there by now. It'll be dark soon, and this place is not safe once the light has gone."

"What do we do if he is not there?" I asked.

"Yes, dear, I was getting to that," replied Winnie,

studying her stitching. "Oh, I seem to have dropped one, dear; hold on..." We watched as she picked up the stitch with her needle and began to cast off before changing her mind and casting a few back on before continuing with a quick rhythmic clicking.

"Get a good night's sleep, and tomorrow, wake early; the earlier, the better, as long as it's light. You'll be needing food. Do you have some?"

"Not much," I confessed. "We only intended to stay for one night and we planned to be almost home by now."

"Home," said Quentin wistfully, "sitting by the fire all together, eating a fine winter's feast with truffles and port."

"It's not a feast by rights, but I've made some bread to take with you," Winnie said proudly, gesturing to the griddle where an uneven loaf lay browning by the fire.

"Thank you so much," I said. "And what would we do in the morning, if we hadn't found Robin, that is?"

"Go back to the old bridge on the lane, but don't cross it. Instead, take a left to the falls; you'll find a stone staircase next to the water. It's very steep and wet, watch your step and you'll be fine. Climb it up to the very top, and you'll reach the meadow. The river that feeds the falls runs down the middle; follow along the bank, and it will take you to the trees, then..."

"It's beginning to get a little complicated," I confessed. "Are you getting this, Quentin?"

"I should draw a map," he said. Taking paper from his satchel and inking up his quill, he set about drawing until he had reached the trees. "I hope it's not much further; I'm running out of paper."

"Then you might need a second page," suggested Winnie, "for I've only just begun. When you get into the trees, you'll see an old standing stone to your left; it has a pattern of swirls carved into it, and that's how you know where you are. Next to the stone is a deer path; it's narrow and a bit overgrown, but don't worry, just follow it up."

She paused and thought to herself for a minute, then reached into her basket. "It can get a bit tricky up there, mind, and you can easily get turned around, so take this wool." She passed over a ball that I held in my hands; the yarn was red and thick. "Pull off a length and tie it to the trees every few feet so you don't get lost, and it will help you on your way down too... Now tuck it down at the bottom of your bag, dear; you don't want it falling out."

She watched carefully as I did as she suggested and nodded in approval before continuing. "The path will lead you right up into the snow line. Don't stop; it's not safe. There are things up there in the trees that are watching. Pay them no heed; they can't harm you if you don't acknowledge them, so keep your mind on the path. When you reach the fork, go left. There's a rocky bit and after that, you'll be in the snow. Do you have good boots, dear?" She looked down toward my feet and nodded again. "They'll do, but you should carry young Quentin; we don't want the frost biting off those pretty toes. The animals use the path, so it's well-marked. Follow their footprints, and they will guide you up to the clearing, and there you'll find Elsie."

Her final comment seemed odd. "Your friend will be waiting for us in the snow?" I asked.

"Yes, dear, and she will be expecting you; she always is."

Quentin shot me a look; he was on his third sheet of paper and had been drawing a map, the name 'Elsie' was at the top of the page.

"Really?" I asked incredulously. "Why will she be there?"

"Oh, she lives there," answered Winnie. "In a little green caravan, she does. When I say little, I mean little for a bear, dear... it's very big to the rest of us."

"A bear!" I gasped. "Winnie, are you suggesting we

spend tomorrow climbing a mountain to visit a bear in the snow?"

"Why yes," replied Winnie, "it's the natural thing to do, dear, if you want to know where he is."

I must have looked puzzled, so she continued, "Now, when you arrive, it will be evening, so plan to stay the night. Don't worry, she has plenty of room."

"Well, it was very nice visiting you..." began Quentin, slipping the papers into his bag and rising to leave.

"Winnie, why do you think this bear can help us?" I asked as I gestured at Quentin to stay.

"Because that's what she does," replied Winnie. "When anything is lost, she knows where to look, and she makes the nicest tea."

"Are you sure it's safe?" I asked. "I've never met a bear before; I hear they can be a bit savage."

"Maybe some are," answered Winnie, "but I've never met one like that. Some can be a bit abrupt, grumpy even, but savage? No. The only creatures that are savage are humans like yourself, but you seem like a kind one."

"I can't argue with you there," I agreed. "I often feel ashamed of my kind, but there are also many good ones."

"They're the ones that matter, dear," replied Winnie, "but as a woodland creature, it's safest to stay clear; I've had more than one friend who died in a trap. They like to wear us as trim, you see, dear."

"Yes, and I'm sorry for that," I said. "That's just horrible."

"My friend in the pond, dear, the one you saw earlier, well, I know she's no more than my own reflection now, but once I had a sister, Millie, and I pretend she's still here with me. We built the dam together, we did, but they came up here and got her, and they turned her into a hat. What use is a hat, I ask you? Something to keep your ears warm, I suppose, but my sister was a lovely one and I miss her every day. Don't fret about Elsie, dear, she'll be happy to help you. I hope you find little Robin waiting at the lodge, but if you don't, set out at first light and follow the map."

She rose and shuffled over to me. "Now bow your head, dearie; this is for you." She placed the scarf she had been knitting around my neck. "This'll keep you warm, just one last row for good measure..." She knitted a little more with a flurry of her needles, then cast off and flicked the end over my shoulder. "Yes, very nice, good colour on you too," she said admiringly.

Quentin looked me over. "Is that a sleeve?" he asked.

I looked down, and indeed, there did seem to be a small, narrow sleeve protruding from the scarf.

"Oh goodness, yes, you get a sleeve into the bargain," said Winnie. "You never know when a sleeve might come in useful; you just never know. Now, let me wrap the bread up for you. It's still warm, and you can pop it into your coat pockets to keep your fingers toasty."

Winnie wrapped the small loaves in squares of cheesecloth and I slipped them into the pockets of my coat, then stood up from the floor. I towered above her, such a busy, round, twinkling creature; she led the way and opened the door, letting in a cold evening wind. Quentin followed me out into the dusk.

"Thank you so much," I said, crouching down. "I'm so very sorry about your sister."

"Don't be sorry, you didn't do it," replied Winnie. "And besides, they are always with you, aren't they?"

"You have been so lovely to us, and I can't think of how to repay you," I said.

"Visit again anytime," said Winnie. "I'll keep the lamp oil burning." She leaned forward and gave me a warm hug, then hugged Quentin, who stood stiff as a board. "Now, get along while you can still see the path. Don't dawdle; it's not safe after dark."

Quentin climbed into the bag, and I lifted it onto my shoulder. Then, waving goodbye one final time, we set out for the lodge.

It was a quiet walk back along the path that ran beside the stream, and I walked a little faster as the light was quickly fading. Quentin looked out into the gloom, but there was no sign of Robin.

As we reached the bridge, it was almost dark, and pale mist hovered over the water beneath it, obscuring the arch so that it looked for all the world like an ornate wall in the forest.

"We are almost back," said Quentin. "I've never been one for praying, but I have turned this bag into a house of worship this last half hour. I'll give anything to have Robin greet us at the door."

"Me too," I agreed. "Perhaps he has been home all day waiting for us."

"Yes," replied Quentin brightly. "He's tucked into the blankets on the sofa where he's made a little nest next to the truffle. Or perhaps he couldn't quite manage to get in through the window and is waiting outside... We'd better hurry. He might be cold."

"Don't worry," I replied. "I'm sure he could easily get in."

"Then yes, he's on the sofa. I can see him there now, and we will play his little song. Though my legs are tired, I'll join him for as long as he likes."

We were up by the bridge where the mist from the river had risen and spread over the lane, and I strained to see as I slowly made my way along. Finally, we rounded the bend and reached the stone gateposts; the little lodge was there, tucked between the trees, and at the window, a weak light flickered.

"He's home!" cried Quentin as I pushed open the door. "Robin, we're back!" but there was no reply.

"Where is he?" implored Quentin. "I don't understand. Did he come in and light the lamp then go out again to find us? I don't understand, I don't understand."

"We left the lamp lit this morning," I explained. "I didn't expect it would burn for this long. Perhaps he did visit and went back out to see where we were."

I went to the table where I had left the cake and note for him, but they were both untouched.

Quentin was watching and saw them too. "He is not here," he whispered. "He's gone."

I set the bag on the sofa, he climbed out, and we sat silently together with the blanket wrapped around us.

The lamp ran out of oil, the room became dark and still.
We must have fallen asleep; I don't remember dreaming.

Chapter Four

Elsie

When I first opened my eyes, I could just make out the shapes of furniture in the room. The window appeared as a pale grey square, and I realised it was morning.

The hearth, without a fire, was a dark chasm, and above it, the hulking head and shoulders of the old boar hung from the wall. There was no comfort here, not without Robin.

Quentin, who had slept beside me, stirred. He ruffled his feathers and opened an eye. "It looks like morning," he said, and he raised his head and looked over at the door. "It's time to go."

His voice was flat and weary. I didn't have the energy to put on a brave face, so I simply nodded and went over to the kitchen to wash my face and collect the food. I didn't have the inclination to make a fire-every moment felt precious-so we drank a cup of cold water between us and prepared to leave.

"Is this a good idea?" asked Quentin as I packed the rucksack. "I really don't know if it is, to be going so far from here, the last place he saw us together."

"I don't know," I replied. "Perhaps we should stay for a little while longer."

We went outside and sat together on the step.

"Robin!" Quentin cried out. "Robin, where are you?" His words drifted off in the cold morning air.

We heard the call of ravens circling in the sky above, but there was no sign of our friend.

Time passed. Without a watch, I cannot say how long, but the weak winter sun was rising, and its cool light began to illuminate the day, and still, there was no sign.

"How long shall we wait?" asked Quentin. "I just don't know what to do."

"Perhaps we should take Winnie's advice," I said. "We can't sit here all day. Why don't you write a note for Robin? We can put it on the table next to the cake and leave the window open so he can come inside."

"Sounds like a plan," Quentin answered wearily, and together we went back into the house.

"Would you mind helping me remove this before we leave?" He asked after he had written the note, and he looked down at his neck. The odd knitted item that Winnie made had ridden up during the night and was bunched under his chin. I went to the kitchen and found a knife, the blade was dull but it only took a few minutes of working it over the wool to make a hole and soon Quentin was free.

I packed up provisions, tied the empty lamp to my rucksack, and we set off. Quentin rode in the carpetbag, and I retraced our steps from the day before. It must have rained in the night, and Robin's prints were gone from the mud. The path curved gently, as the bridge came into view-crumbling limestone, thick with ivy.

Quentin, took out his map. "Take a left," he instructed, "and we'll follow the stream up to the falls."

At first, the water babbled as it rolled past us over the rocks, but as we drew near, the roar was all we heard. The immense shining curtain fell before us, foaming as it plunged into the inky depths of the pool. Steep cliffs of granite, clothed in bright green moss and ferns, rose up sharply on either side.

Quentin inspected his map. "Over there!" he cried and

pointed his wing to a narrow stone staircase that was carved into the rock.

"I hope it's not too slippery," I replied, and my words were carried off by the wind that rose up from the thundering falls.

I picked my way around the water's edge until I reached the first of the steps. It was freezing and wet there, the spray soaked into our clothes and ran down my face, making it hard to see. I looked down at Quentin. Droplets of water had beaded on his feathers and poured from the brim of his little brown hat.

"I can't bear to watch," he cried. "I'm going inside," and his head retracted into the bag.

The stone steps were slippery, I climbed them on my hands and feet, holding on to the ferns as I made my way through the soaking mist-hand and foot, hand and foot-until I grew too tired to think, and in that way, I steadily ascended, farther and farther into the white swirling clouds. My eyes were fixed to the step in front, one after the other, until finally, the mist began to clear, and as we emerged into a field of lush green grass bathed in sunshine. A few final steps and I was up! Standing in the clearing at the top of the falls.

The bag began to move, and Quentin popped out his head and looked around.

"I need to rest," I gasped as I slid to the ground and landed on the cold, wet grass.

"You did a good job, Miss. Well done," he said, and he hopped right out and sat beside me.

From our vantage point, the falls were nothing more than a wide, shallow stream that slipped over the edge in a shining curl of clear water. It was quiet here, with just the sigh of the wind as it danced through the trees that surrounded us.

"Are you hungry?" I asked, taking a small loaf from my pocket and offering it to Quentin.

"Do we have water?" he replied, looking cautiously at the bread. "I need to wet my beak before attempting that."

"Yes, it is a little dry," I agreed, laughing. "Here..." I retrieved a jar from my rucksack and poured a little water into the lid. He took a drink, and when he was done, I placed a piece of broken bread there and filled it again so that it could soak.

"Thank you," said Quentin. "Now take a drink yourself. That climbing was quite the feat! I would never have guessed you'd have it in you."

"Neither would I," I replied. "In fact, I'm still not sure I do. I'm terrified about the prospect of going back down.

There has to be another way..."

I took a long drink of the sweet, cold water and ate. Below us, a thick blanket of white clouds stretched endlessly in all directions. Above us, an eagle circled in the pale blue sky.

"I don't like the look of him," whispered Quentin, tucking in close by my side, and I placed my hand on the soft feathers of his back to comfort him.

"You are safe with me," I said.

In the silence, I felt the breeze caress the grass. It touched my hair with its gentle fingers, and my heart filled with peace. Beside me, Quentin sighed.

"We will be fine, dear friend," I whispered to myself and him together. "We will all be fine."

The clouds beneath us drifted apart, revealing a vista far below. The dark forest that clothed the hillside below gave way to dull green fields divided by the undulating line of a hedgerow.

"Look," I said, pointing down. "There's the path we travelled to the woods."

I traced it back with my finger as it rose up and disappeared behind the back of the hill. "The gate would be there," I said, pointing, "and just out of sight of your home... And down there... yes, look, Quentin, down on the far side, sits Rookscroft!"

"I see it!" cried Quentin. "The side of the house, and the stables at the back. The kitchen door is just around the corner, and inside the kitchen is the old black range and well-stocked pantry... I would give anything to be back there now. If only we could fly like that eagle, we would be home in time for lunch... Robin would be waiting for us, sleeping soundly on our pillow by the fire, with dreams of sea monsters in his little round head."

"That day will come," I said. "I'm sure of it, and we'll look back on this moment with fondness. Is that the sea? I think I can pick out the rooftops of the fishing cottages down there. Perhaps Whittington is in the harbour mending his nets, and Kitty is in the house."

"Reading by the fire," added Quentin. "I'm sure she's the kind that loves to read."

"Perhaps we can invite her to the library?" I suggested. "She's welcome to borrow all the books."

"Yes!" said Quentin. "Robin will be so excited to show her around. He loves books more than anyone! I wish he was here with us now. Wouldn't he just die for this view! I'm sure he could identify every cloud for us... Look how the ones out there are curling like a row of rolling waves."

I looked to where he pointed and saw them drifting over the bay, a perfect row of curls that slowly melted back into the sky.

"We'll tell him about this," I said. "When we're all home again, we'll sit in the kitchen and chat about our adventures."

"But what if..." began Quentin, and he looked at me with a questioning eye.

"He's fine," I said reassuringly. "Now, let's go and find him. My legs feel a bit better, and we have a long way to go. Would you prefer to walk or ride?"

"The bag, please," Quentin answered. "It makes it easier to chat."

He nimbly hopped in, I got to my feet, hoisted him up, and off we set.

"Now I think we follow the river up," he said, looking out over the clearing and indicating with a movement of his beak.

"I think you're right," I agreed, and we followed along its banks across the wide meadow. "I bet this is beautiful in the spring," I said. "I wouldn't be surprised if it isn't filled with lilies. Have you ever seen them growing wild?"

"I can't say I have," replied Quentin. "I've always lived near the house where it's safe, especially after the incident with my family, so I've never seen the wilds before."

"I understand. I am sorry we're here."

"At least we're together, which is some comfort... But what about poor Robin?"

"Oh, he'll be fi..." I began.

"...Please don't do that," interjected Quentin. "It's not fair, you always being so sure that everything will work out, and where does that leave me? Feeling like the sad sack and I'm not the negative kind."

He was right.

"I'm really sorry," I replied. "I was just trying to be strong. Of course, I don't know any more than you, and probably much less. I was just trying to keep our spirits up."

"Well, might I suggest you put that burden down, Miss," Quentin said kindly. "It must be exhausting, and you don't need to carry it on my account. I'm sad, you're sad, we don't know where Robin is, so let's just be sad together. At least it's honest."

"You're right as always," I said as I smiled down at

him. "Thank you."

I took a deep breath, and when I let it go, my hopes and dreams went with it and drifted away on the breeze. Quentin was right. It did feel better to be honestly sad, and I let the heaviness sit with me as I walked along the bank of the river.

We did not speak again until we had reached the far side of the field, and there, by the water's edge, under an old cedar tree, we spotted the stone marker.

"Oh look," Quentin exclaimed as we approached. "This is the stone-you can see the swirl carved into the top, just as Winnie described."

The pillar rose up out of the moss and stones, it stood at waist height and measured a foot across. The snaking curve carved onto its side, spiralled around the top and culminated in a shallow depression filled with water that mirrored the sky.

I dipped my finger in and anointed my forehead and the top of Quentin's hat. "Please grant us safe passage," I whispered to the trees.

"Whatever are you doing?" asked Quentin.

"I don't know, it just felt right, I suppose," I said, gazing up at the narrow path that traced its way upwards through the dense forest. "We need all the help we can get, and I feel this is a holy place."

"Well, I hope you didn't get my hat wet," he said, shaking his head. "Now let's get on-it feels like it's late already."

As improbable as it seemed-we had woken up so early, and surely we couldn't have been travelling for so long-but when I looked around, the light did appear to be fading.

"I think it might be all these trees," I said, "though I can't say for sure, it almost feels like time moves differently here. Are you ready?"

"As I'll ever be," he replied, and we began our slow climb up the steep and crumbling trail.

The forest was anything but silent. A woodpecker paused his hammering and let out a haunting cry. All around us, a constant rustling could be heard, punctuated by the loud quarrelling of ravens who called to each other from every direction.

"It feels very eerie," I whispered.

"They know we are here," replied Quentin.

"What are they saying?" I asked. "Can you

understand?"

"Not every word, but the gist of it is that they do not welcome strangers."

"I'm sorry I asked," I whispered back.

I cleared my throat. "We would like to apologise for disturbing your peace," I said loudly. "We are on a quest, and we need to pass. We mean you no harm."

"They are not afraid of us," hissed Quentin. "I believe it is the other way round."

"Do you think there are dangerous animals here?" I asked, straining to see into the shadows.

"Well, as we are on our way to visit a bear, I think it's safe to assume there are all manner of larger inhabitants," replied Quentin, "and some of them probably not so friendly."

I paused and turned to look back the way we had come, and the path below disappeared into the trees. Quentin noticed it too.

A Path Through the Wild Woods

"It might be time to break out the wool," he suggested.

"Good idea," I replied, and I fished the tightly wrapped ball out from my bag, found the loose end, and drew a little out with my fingers. I broke a length off and tied it around a branch next to the path. The red yarn stood out brightly against the browns and greens of the forest.

"It looks very festive, I must say," commented Quentin.

"It will be easy to see on our way home," I replied, "we should tie some at every bend."

We walked a little further, and at the next turn, I marked a tree with more wool and we continued in this fashion as we made our way along.

We came to a fork in the path and paused to consult the map, "We need to take the left one up the hill," advised Quentin, and I tied a little wool to mark the spot.

After a while, the path turned to the right and continued up a steep rock face. It was an arduous climb with glimpses of the Harvest Moon mountains on the far side of the Salish Sea.

"I don't know how we'll ever get back," I gasped between breaths. "Is this even the way?"

The sky was low and white.

"It looks like snow," said Quentin.

My feet slipped on the rocky soil as I scrambled up on my hands and knees, not daring to look down.

"This doesn't seem like a path," I gasped, pulling myself up onto a large rock. "I need to rest."

I sat for a moment looking out at the view.

"Look, up ahead," said Quentin. "If I'm not mistaken..."

Above us, the rocks ended at a dense line of trees, and there, on a branch, was a length of mustard yellow wool, tied in a bow.

"Winnie was here," I said. "Winnie was here!"

I took a jar of water from my rucksack and poured out a measure for Quentin before drinking myself and we sat for a while until I caught my breath. I looked up to the dark forest above, and as I watched, the snow began to fall.

"It really is magical," I whispered. "I never dreamed I would be so far away."

"Never mind about that, keep your wits about you,"

cautioned Quentin, and as if on cue, a huge bird glided over, white as a cloud, and slowly circled before drifting off toward the north.

"That was odd," I said. "As though you conjured it up. What kind was that? I have never seen anything quite like it before."

"Nor I," replied Quentin. "It looked like a spirit to me and if you hadn't mentioned seeing it, I would have assumed it was a vision."

"Or maybe we're sharing the same dream," I said. "Are you ready to continue?"

I screwed the lid back on the empty jar and packed it away, then picked up the carpet bag and continued our ascent. Snowflakes drifted down like feathers; they did not melt into the dusty ground, but slowly accumulated one by one, carpeting the trail that led us ever upward.

It was growing dark now, and the light had changed from white to an eerie blue. The forest was silent except for the crunch of my feet as I made fresh steps in the pristine snow.

How long we walked I cannot say, but finally, the path curved to the right, and through the trees, a clearing came into view. A snowfield, bathed in soft purple twilight. Toward the back, the orange flames of a campfire flickered, illuminating the steps of an old caravan on which sat a large bear wearing an exquisite costume who waved in welcome.

I paused.

"We still have time to turn back," hissed Quentin. "She's huge!"

I watched her through the fading light, beside the glowing fire.

"And do what?" I asked. "Freeze to death in the forest, or slip off the cliff by the waterfall as we descend in the dark?"

"You have a point," replied Quentin. "At least she's waving."

"If you're scared, go down to the bottom of the bag and I'll put the flap over and button it up."

"I'll stay low," replied Quentin, "but don't bother with the button. I might need to make a speedy exit."

Elsie and Her Caravan

He tucked himself away, down under the blanket so that only the glint of his eye was visible, peering up from the shadows. "I always fancied myself a bit of a spy," he whispered. "You may continue Miss."

I waved back at Elsie with my stomach in a knot, and made my way to her across the vast snowy field. My boots crunched loudly with each step, and I could see my breath in the freezing air. Above, the sky was clearing, and a glowing moon hung low above the trees.

"Hurry, friends," called Elsie, rising from the steps to greet us. "You must be half frozen."

Her voice was low and warm, and the words drifted to me through the winter air.

"It is very cold," I replied as we drew close. "Hello, Elsie. I'm sorry to bother you on such a beautiful night, but we need your help."

"I have been expecting you," she replied. "Come closer to the light and let me see you."

The fire was still between us, and I watched her through the dancing flames as she leaned toward me from the steps. She wore an elaborate hat on her head, flat on top and curled at the sides like the roofline of a Chinese house. Golden trim ran along its edges, and a row of red tassels hung down on cords below her ears.

Around her shoulders, she wore a thick shawl, embroidered with greenery and red poppies, and below that, crinoline skirts as wide as the caravan steps fanned out under a dark wooden skirt.

"Step forward now and don't be shy," she said. I saw the glint of her ivory teeth, and her leathery nose twitched as she sniffed the evening air.

I had never seen a bear before, and I should have been afraid, yet there was something soft and kind in her manner that reminded me of Winnie. Her eyes twinkled as I made my way around the fire and stood before her.

"I apologise for staring," she soothed, "but my sight is not the best. Please do not be offended."

She gazed intently at my face and then her eyes wandered down to the bag. "And welcome to you too," she said. "There is no need to hide. I promise not to bite."

Quentin's head slowly emerged, and he looked up at her. "Well, hello," he replied in his most commanding voice, and I noticed that he had puffed up his neck feathers in an attempt to seem larger.

"Well, let me get you sorted out," said Elsie, and she stepped down toward us. Up close, she was a good foot taller than me, and her clothing made her seem bigger still. Her skirts crinkled as she passed us to inspect a large copper pot that steamed on the coals.

"I hope that pot is not intended for us," Quentin whispered urgently.

"Well, actually, it is," replied Elsie, whose hearing was very good. "I thought you might like a soak, so I put on some water just for you. It is hard to get your bones warm on a cold night like this. Come along to the caravan, come along."

She climbed the steps and went in through the painted door. Quentin shot me a glance-he was afraid, perhaps rightfully so. Was it wise to follow? I didn't know, but there was little choice and when she turned and beckoned I began to climb the steps.

"Come in," she said in her caramel voice. "Come in, come in! Welcome to my home."

The caravan was large and warmly lit. Three good-sized beds were built into the walls, a hooked rug the colour of plums lay over the polished wood floor, and a profusion of pink roses accented with gold decorated the cream clapboard walls. The window frames and trim around the beds were also gilded, and each bed was covered in a patchwork blanket and pillows the colour of a garden in bloom.

Towards the back, on the right side, was a little

kitchen where rows of labelled jars sat neatly on a wooden shelf above a sink dressed with a gathered curtain that grazed the floor. To the right, next to the stove, was a small cupboard, and from this, Elsie took two towels and two tin pans, one large and deep and the other fit for a toy.

"Make yourself comfortable on the bed here," she said, patting the quilt. "Take off your boots, and I'll fetch the water to soak your feet. They must be freezing."

"We don't have time for soaking our feet," snapped Quentin. "We're here on urgent business, and we came here for your help, then we must leave."

Elsie smiled kindly and leaned over towards him. "Little friend, you are safe here, and it is almost dark," she said. "Stay for the night-it has been a long day. Once you are settled, I will do a reading, but the leaves need your calm focus if you are to ask them a question."

"Thank you, Elsie," I replied. "You're right. We've had a very long day, and we really do welcome your hospitality. Winnie sent us to you, we are searching for-"

She raised her large paw and pressed a claw to her mouth. "Shhhh," she whispered. "The leaves are listening-let them tell the story. Oh yes dear Winnie, she and I are great friends, now sit back while I fetch the water."

I took a seat on the bed and sank onto the thick mattress piled with pillows. It smelt of rose and lavender and I closed my eyes and imagined summer. The bag was beside me, its mouth open wide, and Quentin gingerly stepped out onto the quilt.

"We are done for now," hissed Quentin. "There's no escape, and here we are, trapped by a bear."

"We're fine," I replied. "She's a friend of Winnie's. Now settle down. Isn't this bed cosy?"

Elsie returned carrying a pot. "Quick, take off your wet socks," she instructed as she poured the steaming water into a pan on the floor. "Put your feet in while it's warm." She turned her attention to Quentin. "And as for you, young man... Let me balance your little pan on the edge of the bed, and there... That should do it. Now step in and warm your toes."

Quentin gingerly lowered his feet into the water. "Oh, that feels nice," he sighed. "I can feel the life returning."

I slowly eased my cold feet into the pan. It was almost uncomfortable at first, but after a few moments my toes began to warm and the water felt lovely. I leaned back into the pillows and thanked Elsie, who was busy at the kitchen sink.

"You are welcome," she replied without turning. "I

have been waiting for you all afternoon. I was beginning to worry that something had happened-it was getting so late-but now you are here, everything is fine."

"How did you know we were coming?" I asked.

"It's the leaves," replied Elsie, holding up a tin. "The leaves and the trees they always know. Now let's get you fed. Do you both like soup and bread? That's what I live on most days."

"Sounds lovely," I replied.

"Good," answered Elsie. "I'll put the pot on," and without another word, she shuffled back out to her campfire.

"I hope it's not meat-in the soup, I mean," whispered Quentin as we watched her wide body silhouetted against the flames.

"Whatever it is, let's be grateful," I replied. "Beggars can't be choosers, and we can't find poor Robin if we don't eat."

"Well, it doesn't feel right eating a fellow creature," replied Quentin, shaking out his neck feathers. "Just the thought of it sends a chill right down my spine."

"Even bugs?" I asked. "I see you scratching for them

outside, or are you just looking for new friends?"

"Bugs?" asked Quentin. "Oh, bugs, yes, they are a different thing entirely. Simple, delicious, especially the ripe ones... I don't eat the butterflies without saying a quick prayer first-they are really too beautiful to snack on-but sometimes the urge to pluck them from the sky overcomes me."

"Well, that's a strange thing to do, and slightly gruesome if you ask me. I'm not sure what the soup is, so let's just be grateful and not ask questions."

Elsie returned with a large iron cauldron, which she placed next to the sink. A delicious aroma rose from it and filled the room, waking my stomach, which grumbled loudly.

"Sounds like it warmed up just in time," laughed Elsie, and she lifted three bowls from the shelf and began to fill them with a wooden spoon. "This will fill our bellies-it's made with carrots and sweet potatoes."

"Do they grow wild here?" I asked as she handed me a bowl.

"Wild? No, but I brought some seedlings with me when I first came here, and they grow back every year in my garden," she replied.

She laid Quentin's little bowl on the bed beside him and made herself comfortable in an old armchair.

I tasted the soup; it was sweet and thick.

"Very nice," commented Quentin after taking a sip. "I am relieved that you are a vegetarian."

"Vegetarian?" laughed Elsie. "Whatever gave you that idea? I don't turn my nose up at a good piece of meat or the occasional fish, but mostly, I eat from my garden."

"And do you eat birds?" asked Quentin cautiously. "I have heard some find them tasty, but the pheasants are often considered too gamey-especially the older ones. Did I mention I'm two? That's way past my prime."

"There is no need to worry," replied Elsie with a chuckle. "Eat up, eat up! Would you like some bread to dip in? I'll go and fetch you some." She put down her bowl and went back to the kitchen where a crusty loaf was resting under a cloth.

"Try this," she said, tearing off a generous chunk and handing it to us. "I made it this morning."

I broke the bread in two and placed a little in both our bowls, and we hungrily ate every bite.

When we had finished, Elsie rose, took our plates to

the sink, then emptied our foot baths and brought back a rough towel to dry our feet. "Give them a good rub to get the blood going," she advised. Then she slipped out to the fire and returned moments later with warm socks for me and a wool blanket for Quentin, which she tucked around his toes.

"Now you are all fed and comfortable, let me make us tea. Just a minute, while I get the stove going and put the kettle on."

We watched as she filled the iron kettle and placed it on the range, poked the fire back to life, then carefully took down three cups and a heavy earthenware teapot and placed them on the table that she had set before us.

"I can't drink so much tea before bed," gasped Quentin. "Why, I'll be up all night!"

"I have a little cup that's perfect for you," Elsie replied.

She gathered three painted tins from above the sink, took a silver spoon, and one at a time, took a heaping scoop of dark leaves from each one and added them to the pot.

"Hold it securely in both hands," she instructed, handing the tea pot over "and give it a nice, slow swirl to mix the leaves together."

I did as she asked and passed it back over to her waiting paws. "Now we are going to steep the leaves," she said.

She went to the stove and slowly poured in boiling water from a black kettle until the pot was almost full, and a fragrant smell of tea wafted through the room.

"What kind of tea do you use?" asked Quentin. "It smells familiar, like Earl Grey, but there is something more-something earthy."

"That will be the Lapsang Souchong. I make my own with pine resin and needles. I can give you some to take with you if you would like me to. Would you care for a biscuit?"

"I never turn my beak up at a biscuit," replied Quentin.

She shuffled back to the cupboard and returned with a round black tin decorated with painted flowers. Inside were small, hard biscuits. I took out one for each of us.

"How do you take your tea?" asked Elsie, looking down at Quentin.

"Usually a shallow cup or saucer works best," replied Quentin, "but I can manage with anything you have handy."

"That will be perfect," replied Elsie, "as my reading cups are exactly as you describe, and I have a very sweet one that's just your size."

She went to the cupboard once more and brought out shallow china cups. They were plain white with dainty handles.

"I cannot drink from them myself," she admitted. "My paws are far too large, but they were gifted to me with this caravan many years ago by the goat lady who lived here all her life."

"The goat lady?" asked Quentin. "Was she actually a goat?"

"No," laughed Elsie. "She was a goat herder. Her family lived up here for a hundred years. She was born in this caravan, in that very bed, and most everything you see belonged to her. She taught me so many things while she was here, and when she left this earth and went back to the stars, she left it all to me."

"How did you meet?" I asked, but Elsie shook her head.

"Now that is a story for another time," she said. "There are more important questions you need answers to tonight. Now please sit back and close your eyes, take a deep breath in through the top of your head, and observe it move all the way down your body and out through the bottom of your feet... Slowly, slowly, yes, that's the way. Now again, and again, and again... Now open your eyes."

And there before us were three cups of clear, hot tea.

Elsie slowly dipped a biscuit into hers. "It's piping hot, too hot to drink, but a good time to soak a biscuit," she suggested.

We followed her lead, and the tough little biscuits turned soft and sweet in the hot brown drink.

"Oh, I like these," said Quentin. "Now Robin loves..." He caught himself and sat, stirring the biscuit absently in his tea until a large part detached and sank to the bottom. "Oh dear," he whispered. "I think I've broken it."

Elsie looked over and smiled. "Oh, that's fine," she said. "You can drink around it. Would you like another?"

"No, thank you, but I ruined the reading," said Quentin sadly. "Shall we start again with a fresh cup?"

"It's just how it's meant to be," Elsie reassured him. "Now drink up, but leave just a little in the bottom, and we can begin."

As I sipped my drink, I thought of little Robin, and my stomach tightened knowing he was out there on this cold spring night. I looked over at Quentin, and I knew he was thinking the same. All our love and sadness, our hope and fear, moved through our hands and into the tea.

"Now take the cup by the handle with your left hand and move it in a quick circle three times," instructed Elsie. We did as she said, and some of the leaves clung to the sides while others stayed at the bottom in the liquid. "Good, that's right. Now tip the cup over the saucer... that's it... slowly now... yes, you can take your hand away and let it rest for a moment."

We looked up at Elsie and waited. "Now I want you both to think about what you would like to ask the leaves," she continued. "Think very hard-what are you looking for, what will your future be?"

I thought of little Robin dancing to his song, sitting on the bed back home, talking about the clouds, enjoying a dust bath, and tears sprang to my eyes. I looked over at Quentin and he was crying too, the tears fell from his yellow eyes and ran down the feathers of his cheeks.

"Don't despair," whispered Elsie kindly. "Now turn your cups over, and we will see what we will see."

I passed my cup into Elsie's waiting paws, and she inspected it carefully before tipping it toward me. "Now the handle represents you," she explained, "so you are here," she tapped the handle with the tip of her claw, "the rim up here is what is happening now, the sides are the next few days, and the leaves at the bottom of the cup are your future."

I nodded, and she tilted the cup back to take a better view, turning it in her large paws and pausing to scratch her head.

"Well, this is an interesting one," she said almost to herself. "The cup talks in riddles, and its story is true but not always clear, so I'm going to tell you what I see. Be still and hear me out, and please don't be alarmed."

She considered the cup for a quiet moment more, then looked me full in the eye. "You are looking for someone," she said finally, "and in the future, I see a bird flying high over the tops of the trees, the dark forest, a journey home. A house, yes, a house and the sea."

"I'm sorry," she said after further inspection, "but I cannot see your little friend." She passed the cup back and shifted her attention to Quentin. "I believe this means the world to you," she said kindly. "Pass over your cup now, and let me see what I can find."

Elsie took the little cup from his long yellow fingers. "Now think of your friend and let your heart go to him," she instructed.

Quentin closed his eyes, and Elsie considered the

leaves. "Mmm," she said quietly and slowly scratched her head below her ear as she thought. "Mmm, very interesting. Take a look..."

She tipped the cup toward us, and when we looked inside, the wet biscuit dough had settled to form a triangle of pale yellow on the side of the cup that came to a point just below the rim.

"This is the mountain," said Elsie, "and you are here right at the top." She took back the cup, studied it some more and her eyes brightened. "And here is your friend," she said excitedly. "Look, he is a small bird, is he not?"

She tipped back the cup and pointed to a little patch of leaves about halfway down, almost obscured by the biscuit, and there was a tea leaf that looked a little like a quail.

"But what does this mean?" cried Quentin. "Is he buried in the mountain? Is he dead?" and his eyes began to swim.

Elsie Holding Quentin's Cup

"Take a breath," said Elsie. "He is in the mountain, under the ground, but I do not see death's face."

"Your cup shows the journey that you must undertake. It is a long road, and you are only now at the start, but in the end, I see a book and a serpent. Does this mean something to you?"

"THAT'S ROBIN'S BOOK!" cried Quentin. "Don't you remember, Jayne? The book he was reading before we left and the sea serpents he was so afraid of?"

"Yes," I replied. "Yes, yes, I do! If only we had stayed there and read about adventures instead of coming here."

"I feel he will be found," said Elsie thoughtfully, "though whether you will be reunited, I cannot say."

"I don't understand," I said, "but to know he is alive at least gives us hope."

"Yes," agreed Quentin. "And if he's alive, we'll find him, and I'll never let him out of my sight again. I swear he's too precious for this life."

Elsie took one last look at the cup. "He is not alone," she said as she placed it back on the saucer. "I see others with him."

"Oh no! Is he in danger? Is it foxes?" cried Quentin,

staring wildly.

"Foxes, no. They seem to be about his size," replied Elsie, pointing towards the leaves.

"Don't fret," I said. "A fox would have eaten him by now." And as soon as the words left my mouth, I regretted them.

"I can't lose anyone else to these woods," Quentin whispered, and tears filled his eyes once again. "I swore after my family was lost that I would never trust my heart to another, but Robin... Please, not Robin."

He looked up at Elsie, who answered him with her steady gaze.

"I can't lie," she said calmly. "I see that he is alive, but your future, my friend, is uncertain, and I cannot tell if you will meet again in this life. Such is our journey, that the smallest choice can lead us down a different path, and where that leads, we cannot know."

"Please don't speak in riddles," said Quentin, wiping his eyes with the tip of his wing. "I don't have the strength for them. We came here hoping for an answer, and now my mind is more confused than before. We might have been better staying down by the lodge. Perhaps he didn't wander far. He might even be back there listening to his favourite song. We should go."

"Don't be silly," replied Elsie in her slow and easy way. "It is dark, and he is safe. My advice is that you stay here and get a good night's rest. In the morning, I will send you off with provisions. Now, Quentin, let me fetch you a tincture; it was my mother's recipe."

Elsie went to her cupboard again and brought out a bottle filled with golden oil. She pulled out the cork, put several drops in a little tin cup, then added a teaspoon of brandy, and brought it over.

"Now sip on this till it's gone," she instructed.

"What is it?" I asked, as Quentin wet his beak and took a first tentative swallow.

"Golden root, skullcap, a little valerian root, and honey," she replied. "Would you like a little too? I think I might make one for myself; it's been a long day."

She went back over and prepared us both a little cup. It tasted of herbs, sweet honey, and apple brandy with a slight earthy aftertaste.

"Thank you, Elsie, it's delicious," I said. "Don't you agree, Quentin?"

He didn't reply, and when I looked over, I saw that his eyes were almost closed. I carefully tucked the blanket around him and gently stroked the feathers on his neck as he drifted off to sleep.

"Thank you, he needed that, poor thing," I said. "He lost his entire family in these woods, and now Robin."

"Lost his family?" Elsie asked.

"Yes," I said, "on an ill-advised day trip to the bay, and apparently, not one of them returned."

"That is very sad indeed," she replied, lowering her head. "These woods are no place for ground birds, no place for anyone but forest folk and even then... I didn't want to scare him but his future is uncertain. I advise you to keep your wits about you and don't let him out of your sight. Head back down tomorrow while it's light, keep your eyes on the trail and your mind on home. Once you get below the waterfall, you will be safer; the larger creatures rarely travel down that far."

This sounded ominous indeed.

"His future is uncertain? Is he in danger?" I whispered urgently.

"Now that, I cannot tell," she replied. "The leaves at the bottom of his cup were all over-lots of paths... lots of dead ends. I've never seen that before."

There was a knot in my stomach, and I felt that I

might cry. I looked down at him on the bed, curled up and comfortable, dreaming of something I hoped was pleasant.

"Drink up," said Elsie. "All is not lost, just take great care and do as I say. Now tuck down under the quilt and make yourself cosy. It gets cold here at night, once the stove goes out." I did as she suggested and closed my eyes. The sheets smelt of summer, that's the last thing I remember.

The noise of clanking china and the smell of wood smoke woke me. I squinted about-I was alone in the caravan. The door was open, and outside, the morning sun shone brightly on the snowy field. Elsie was by the campfire.

She busied herself between stirring an iron pot that hung over the flames and wrapping something in a large dried leaf, which she folded into a neat parcel. I noticed that Quentin was gone from the bed, and looking out, I saw that he sat just to Elsie's left, on the far side, and they were talking.

I rubbed my eyes and sat up. The air was cold, so I wrapped the quilt around my shoulders and made my way out to join them, slipping on my boots at the step and walking carefully in Elsie's footprints through the snow. They turned as I approached.

"Well, hello, sleepyhead," Quentin teased. "Nice of you to finally join us. Come and have some tea and a bite to eat; the day's half over already."

I looked toward the sky where, just above the treetops, the pale disc of sun shone through a low veil of thin clouds.

"It can't be that late," I replied. "The sun is hardly up. You seem chipper this morning."

"It was a good night's sleep" replied Quentin "and knowing that Robin is somewhere safe, now we just have to go back down and find him."

"Come and sit here," said Elsie, patting the tree stump by her side, "and I will pour you some tea."

I joined them by the fire and watched the flickering flames dance around the pot. "Would you like some porridge?" asked Elsie, picking up a bowl.

"I would love some," I replied.

"It really sticks to your ribs," said Quentin, "and I mean that in a good way."

Elsie ladled out a thick grey mass and plopped it into the bowl, added a spoon of honey, and passed it over. It didn't look appealing, but Quentin was right-it was very filling, and once the honey was well stirred in, quite tolerable.

"Well, at least we will be heading downhill today," said Quentin brightly, "so it shouldn't be too hard on the legs. We made it up here in a day; if we get a move on, we will be back at the waterfall by early afternoon."

"I like that plan," I replied, "and from there, we can search for Robin. Who knows, he may have found his way back to the lodge by then."

"Let's hope so," said Quentin wistfully, and he looked toward the sky. "I promise never to ask for anything ever again, but please, please let him be there waiting for us at the window."

I ate the rest of my breakfast in silence, and once I was done, I took the quilt back into the caravan, slipped on my coat, and gathered my things.

"Put this in your pocket," said Elsie, handing over the package I had watched her make. "It's just a little food to help you on your journey. Now make your way down quickly and once you get to the field above the falls you can take a rest and eat. The water in the stream there is pure and good to drink. You will need to keep your wits about you as you climb down the rock steps; the mist makes them very slippery."

"I will," I replied. "I'm not looking forward to that part at all. Thank you so much for your help, Elsie. I'd love to see you again sometime. Do you ever travel down past the forest? Our home is just off the lane that runs along the ridge of the hill; it's to the right, overlooking the sea. We'd love you to visit."

"Perhaps," replied Elsie. "I'm not much for travelling anymore, but I wouldn't rule it out. It would be nice to see you both again too -and hopefully your friend."

"Wouldn't that be lovely," I said. "You are welcome any time. Once you're on the path, you can't miss the house; it's the only one there. There's an orchard to the left and an orangery at the back. And if you visit, please feel free to come right in through the kitchen door-we're often back there, and we never use the locks. In fact, I don't even know where the key is anymore."

"Thank you for the invitation," replied Elsie. "I will bear it in mind. Now you had better get going while the day is still young."

She gave me a hug, and as she did, I wished that she was joining us on our journey down. It felt very safe around Elsie.

"Thank you for the reassurances," said Quentin. "I'm sure we'll find Robin thanks to you. Now don't forget our invitation."

She scooped him up in a generous hug, then placed him on the ground and he hopped right into the waiting bag.

"This is for your journey" she said as she tucked a small package in beside him.

I hoisted the rucksack onto my back and the strap of the carpet bag over my shoulder, and with a final goodbye, we set off back across the snowy field.

When we reached the path on the far side, I turned to see her one last time. She was bent over, tending to her fire but she must have sensed me watching and she looked up and waved her paw high in the air.

I waved back with both arms. "Goodbye," I called out. "I hope we meet again."

She nodded twice as if to agree and then returned to her work.

"Well, here we go I suppose," I said to Quentin, "Next stop the lodge" and I turned toward the tunnel of trees that marked the path back home.

Elsie

Chapter Five

The Journey Down

"This shouldn't take too long," said Quentin as I stepped onto the trail, "and if we're quick, we'll be back at the lodge before lunch... I hope Elsie packed something good. I'm crossing my fingers for currant bread."

"Hold that thought," I suggested. "I'm not sure she has access to currants, but I promise to make you a big loaf as soon as we get home."

"Home, yes..." replied Quentin wistfully. "Say, is this the right way?"

I looked ahead, scouring the snowy branches with my eyes. "I don't remember where we left the last thread," I admitted. "Do you?"

"Oh, but look, there are your footprints," said Quentin,

gesturing towards the snow. "If we can follow them back, we can't possibly go wrong."

"After the luck we've had so far, anything's possible," I laughed.

We followed the prints down the trail until the snow thinned and faded from the path, and I began to look for the red wool in the trees.

"I think we should see some soon," said Quentin, reading my mind. "Perhaps around the next bend?"

The path narrowed slightly and dipped as it turned downhill, and as we rounded the corner, I caught sight of a piece of red wool hanging from a branch. "Oh, here it is," I said with relief. "You were right, thank goodness. I was beginning to worry."

"Well, at least we are starting out right," replied Quentin reassuringly. "I seem to remember it was pretty straightforward getting up here, so it should be the same going down."

"Do you think we should remove them as we go?" I asked. "After all, it's not nice to litter."

"Yes, let's," replied Quentin. "They look a bit messy, don't they? We really should take them home with us."

I untied the knot and slipped the woollen strand into my pocket, then turned my attention further back to the trail, and further down, at the bend was a second flash of red.

"Well, we're really on our way now!" said Quentin brightly. "I can't wait to be back at the house, sitting by the fire, with a big slice of cake and a spot of tea..."

"...And you and Robin will be reading a book together, or at least looking at the pictures. Isn't it funny when he sees those fantastical sea creatures? How he fluffs himself up to look bigger."

Quentin didn't reply at first. "We will find him, won't we?" he asked sadly. "Only I couldn't live..." and his words trailed away.

"We won't stop until we've found him," I replied. "Elsie says that he's alive, so we just have to work out where he is. Hang on a second while I untie this one..." We had reached the next piece of wool, which I removed and tucked into my pocket.

Quentin craned his neck. "Look right down there, at the next bend," he cried. "Is that the next thread already?"

"Why, I believe it is," I replied. "But don't you think it seems a little odd? I really don't remember tying on so many."

"I don't either," he agreed. "But we were chatting on the way up, so who can say? Perhaps time is going faster this way. We are going downhill, after all. I suspect we're covering a lot of ground."

I hurried down. It was tied quite high on a branch. "I don't remember reaching up like this to tie it on," I said as I strained to grasp it. "Do you remember me on my toes like this? It was only yesterday."

"I can't say that I do," replied Quentin. "It does seem a little odd. What was in that tincture last night? Does this path seem different to you?"

"Maybe we are imagining things," I said. "This forest has got us all turned round, and I think our minds are playing tricks."

I paused and looked back from where we had come. The path snaked up between the trees, and the snowy patches were gone. I turned to look downhill, and the scene seemed strange and unfamiliar. "I think it's an optical illusion," I concluded (though I wasn't sure). "Walking uphill, our eyes were drawn towards the sky, and it feels more open that way, but downhill we are seeing the path disappearing into the darkness of the woods, which frankly is a bit off-putting. I think we're fine. Let's carry on."

I was about to continue when I got the eerie sense that

someone was watching from the silent trees.

"Look," hissed Quentin, "up there." I saw a flash of bottle green on the side of a fir tree, high above.

"What is it?" I whispered. "I can't..."

A shadowy form dropped from the tree and spread its vast dark wings, it silently coasted over our heads, swooping down along the trail and disappeared around the bend.

"What was that?" hissed Quentin in a panic. "I saw it stare down at us as it flew over. It means to harm us."

"That was rather terrifying," I agreed. "But I think it's gone."

My heart was racing.

"No, it's waiting for us at the bend," stammered Quentin. "I'm going for cover." He withdrew his head and vanished under the woollen blanket.

I clutched the bag tight with both hands and carefully continued downhill. It was steeper here, with half-buried rocks that pushed through the sandy soil, and it took some effort not to trip.

"Do you see more wool?" I asked. "Only I'm not sure

we are on the right path."

I stopped for a moment, and Quentin raised his head and looked around. "Good God, it's there!" he hissed.

"Who?" I asked, frantically looking about.

"Up there... LOOK!"

High above our heads perched a great horned owl, staring down with its huge orange eyes. Its face bore no expression; I could not detect a personality of any kind. It simply looked at us, impartially, without fear.

"Quentin, get back down. I'm going to secure you in," I said. My heart was in my mouth as I buttoned the flap. I never took my eye off the bird.

It did not move but just stared down with an unfathomable gaze. Why it wore a cap and goggles, I did not know.

"Hello," I called out.

Victor

It stared down unblinking and my stomach twisted in a knot, but it was unwise to show fear. I decided to ignore it, to show it that I was not afraid and I looked away.

"Suit yourself," I called out and began to resume my walk.

It swooped down low, grazing the top of my head with its wings, and flew into the trees. My heart thumped in my chest; I had never been so unnerved by a creature before. "You don't scare me," I cried. "Leave us alone!"

The forest fell silent.

I continued along, with my head held high, pretending to be brave and made my way down the trail until I believed that it was gone.

"I think we're safe for now," I said, lifting the flap and looking down at Quentin. "Can you pop up and help me, please? I could do with a second set of eyes. I haven't seen any wool for a while, and I have no idea where we are."

Quentin raised his head over the rim, just high enough to see over. "I'm going to stay low," he explained. "That thing, it lives here, and it's probably stalking us. I'm glad that Robin is underground. I wish I was there with him right now, I truly do."

"Well, stay low but keep your eye out," I suggested,

and I continued our descent through the trees.

I tried to steer my mind away from the fears of the forest by dreaming of home. I was in the kitchen, safe and warm, bored perhaps and contemplating a walk to the village where we could sit and watch the sailboats from the dock. I wondered what Whittington and Kitty were up to. I glanced upward; the treetops waved gently in the pale white sky. No shadows, it would be a good day for fishing. Perhaps Whittington was out on his boat, and Kitty? I had heard that she had started a message service between islands with a bottle post that ran on the tides. She might be on the sand, collecting them now, and then she would head home for an afternoon in town. I could see it all in my mind's eye: the cobbled square, with its crowd of little shops, a chilly day in early spring. Perhaps there were flowers... Yes, there would be flowers...

There was something in the tree above. The huge owl stared silently down, and my heart felt like it had stopped.

"What do you want?" I shouted sternly. It made no reply but kept me in its steady sights.

I continued walking. "Stay low," I whispered urgently. "I'll..."

Without a sound, it was on us, digging its talons into the strap of the carpet bag and lifting it from my shoulder. I twisted around wildly, holding on with both hands as the owl tore it from my shoulder.

"LET GO!" I screamed.

The beating of its huge wings, just inches from my face, made it hard to see, but I could make out its eyes, round and shining, and the sharp beak between them opened. "M-I-N-E," it hissed.

With all my strength, I pulled the bag toward me. There was a tearing sound, the flap flew open, and Quentin tumbled out, landing at my feet, his eyes wild with terror. I threw myself over him, and spread my coat over us with my arms, tucking my head under so it formed a tent-like cover.

I could hear a wild flapping above. "TRAP, TRAP," cried the owl, and then there was silence.

I lay on the ground, curled over my friend. Minutes passed, and my breath began to slow. The damp earth smelt wholesome. Sharp fir needles pricked my skin. An earwig walked across my arm.

Victor Fighting for the Carpet Bag

Time passed slowly in the silent forest.

"I think it's gone," I whispered to Quentin, and I lifted the edge of my coat to look.

It was there, just feet away, trying to dislodge its claws which were caught up in the strap. It realised I was watching and turned to stare with its unflinching gaze, then turned back and continued to tear at the canvas with its sharp, pointed beak.

I pulled the coat back over my head, and Quentin looked up at me with a questioning horror.

"It's still there," I whispered. "I think it's stuck."

We listened, waiting for what felt like an hour until finally there was the sound of whirling air, then silence.

I peeked out from under the coat. On the path lay the carpet bag, torn in two.

I started to stand.

"Don't leave me," cried Quentin in a weak, high voice.

"Of course not," I said, and I scooped him up and wrapped my coat around us both.

The handle of the bag was torn apart, the woollen

blanket lay next to it on the path, and beside that was Quentin's little satchel and the small package wrapped in a leaf that Elsie had added. I folded the blanket and put it in my rucksack along with his little satchel, then picked the package off the ground and carefully unwrapped it. Inside was a small bottle filled with golden liquid, and tied to the bottle was a label.

"A fortifying tincture for times of stress'," I read out loud.

"I think now might be the time for a swig of that," replied Quentin. "If this isn't a time of stress, I don't know what is..."

"You're right," I agreed, removing the lid. "You should go first."

I held the bottle and slowly poured the liquid into his open beak, pausing at intervals until he waved me off with his wing. It was half gone.

"I feel better already," he said. "Now you take the rest."

I did as he suggested and drank the rest of the thick, sweet liquid. It tasted similar to the tincture from the night before, but this one had a spicy taste that warmed my throat.

"It's nice," I said once the last drop was gone. "Would

you like some food too?"

"I think I'll wait until we reach the field," replied Quentin. "It can't be far now, we just need to get to that flat stone we rested on yesterday, and once we've climbed down the rocks past that, we'll be almost there."

"And from there we just go down by the falls and we'll be at the lodge," I replied cheerfully as I resumed walking. "And once we reach it..."

"...Robin could be waiting," said Quentin gayly. "He might even have lit the fire; it would be so nice to be there together, all safe and warm. Were there logs still in the hearth?"

"Yes," I replied. "I'm pretty sure there were, though I told him not to play with matches."

"Tomorrow we will go home together," continued Quentin, his voice rising with excitement. "We will be there by tea time, and that currant bread you promised."

"Won't that be splendid," I replied (the tincture was having an effect on me too, and the forest almost seemed to be tinged with a friendly amber). "Yes, I'll make the biggest loaf you've ever seen, and I have some cherry jam."

"...and Robin can tell us all about his adventures,"

continued Quentin. "Say, shouldn't we be at that rock by now?"

He was right. We had walked very far along the path, and it must have been past noon, yet still, we were in the depths of the forest. But thanks to the tincture, we felt no fear.

"See there," said Quentin, pointing his wing. "I think that's what we are looking for."

I hurried down to the spot where a thread of red wool hung from a branch and began to untie it.

"This is a bit of a puzzle," commented Quentin as I picked at the wool with my fingers.

"Puzzle?" I asked.

"The puzzle is, which way do we go?" answered Quentin, and as I looked, I realised that the tree sat at an intersection of two paths that both continued down the hill.

It took me a moment to think it out. "Well, as I'm left-handed, I'm going to guess I would have tied the wool to a branch on the left of the path," I said. "So we would have come up this path." I pointed to our right.

"But if you remember, you also tied wool on branches

to the right," replied Quentin. "And in that case, we could have come up this path, which seems more familiar to me." He peered about inspecting the trees.

"I'm really not sure," I conceded. "But they both seem to lead back down, so how far wrong could we go?"

"Quite far, I imagine, if our luck so far is anything to go by," replied Quentin. "If we take the wrong one, we're unlikely to be at the cottage by dark, and you remember what Elsie said."

"Only too well," I replied. "This is a quandary. Why don't we sit down and think it over? I'm tired, and I'd like to eat."

We found a wide log and sat there together, facing down the hill. Quentin's feathers were radiant against the dark green of the forest; he stood out like a jewel. I should never have come here with my beloved friends. He turned to look up, and his yellow eyes shone below the wide rim of his hat. I could see his beak moving; he was speaking... "Are you alright?" he asked. "Only you look a bit misty."

"I'm fine," I replied, pulling myself together. "I think I'm just tired." I wanted to tell him how much he and Robin meant to me, but the moment slipped away.

"Now, which path shall we pick?" I asked, pulling

myself together.

"The one to the left," replied Quentin confidently. "I swear I recognise the foliage."

"OK, let's try that one. Shall we eat first? It feels like it's past lunchtime."

I retrieved Elsie's package from my pocket and carefully unfolded the leaf. Inside, I found a lovely round of flatbread made from whole grains, folded over carrots pickled in apple vinegar and a creamy paste made from pine nuts. I broke off a generous corner for Quentin and filled his cup with water before tucking in to eat, and together we sat enjoying our lunch in the quiet of the trees.

After we had eaten, I cleared up our things.

"Are you ready?" I asked.

"As ever," he replied.

"Would you like me to carry you?" I held out my arms.

"Don't you dare even think about putting me down," he said. "I might be half giddy from the tincture, but that doesn't mean I have forgotten that owl."

"It was rather strong; I felt it too. Now are you sure

about the left?" I asked.

"I tend to pick the right over the wrong, unless the wrong is more fun," replied Quentin impishly, "and in this case, I don't think there is much fun to be had down either path, and I believe the left one is the right choice."

So off we set down the left-hand path that wound steeply down through the pines.

"This tincture really is quite something," I said. "Does everything look a little different to you?"

"As if perfused in a golden light? Yes," replied Quentin. "And I have to say that right now I haven't a care in the world. My, it does look different when you're walking back down."

We were standing at the top of a rock face, and from our vantage point, we could see out across the water to the Harvest Moon Mountains. Today they looked closer, and the path seemed much steeper than the day before.

"It really does," I agreed, "and I really don't like heights. I think I'm going to have to clamber down on my bum so I don't slip off the edge."

"Pop me down and I'll lead the way," suggested Quentin brightly. "I fancy a bit of rock hopping. Aren't those mountains well named? They look so autumnal today... and so does the sky."

Somehow everything felt odd and surreal, and as I slowly descended between the rocks, I felt a sense of calm, which was unusual considering my mortal fear of heights. Quentin hopped nimbly ahead, humming a tune as he skipped down the cliff face, oblivious to any danger.

"This is an adventure! I'm even doing a spot of climbing," he called back. "I can't wait to tell Robin all about it. Why, I've never felt so bold."

"You do make it look effortless, unlike me," I laughed.

"You're not doing so badly yourself Miss. Channel your inner mountain goat," he chided, pausing to watch me inch my way down the side of a large boulder.

"That's the way!" he cried excitedly. "Now hurry it up and we'll be back to the lodge in no time."

We descended into the trees where the land flattened out onto a trail.

"Are you sure we came this way?" I asked. "I really don't remember rocks like these."

"I can't say that I do either," admitted Quentin. "But let's keep going; I'm sure we're almost to the falls."

I looked to our left where daylight shone through the branches, and spotted a clearing on the other side of the trees. "I don't remember seeing that before," I said.

"Neither do I," agreed Quentin. "I'm getting the feeling we might be lost. We should go and take a look."

"Yes, let's," I said, and I followed my friend to the edge of the open field. "I'm going to tie some wool around the tree so that we can find our way back to the path," I explained.

"Good idea, even if it's the wrong one... The path, that is," replied Quentin.

I tied on two pieces to be on the safe side while Quentin ran ahead, hopping from one log to the next. "This is very exciting!" he called back. "Hurry along now, Miss, and stop your dawdling. We have an adventure to get on with; Robin's waiting for us somewhere."

I followed as quickly as I could, climbing over logs and moss-covered boulders.

"I'm heading to the top for a better view," he shouted, indicating with his wing. "Come along now, speed it up a bit." He was quite far ahead of me now, and he began to call out to Robin in a strange, exotic cry as he ran along. At the top of the clearing, he stopped and waited for me on a stump.

"It will all work out fine," he said confidently as I approached. "Is the sun setting already? It seems so light, but the sky has the warm glow of sunset if I'm not mistaken."

I reached him and turned to see; everything appeared to be tinged orange, even the grass was bathed in an otherworldly light.

"I think it might be the tincture," I suggested. "I feel as though I'm wearing tinted glasses. I think we drank a little more than recommended."

As I took in the view, I was quite overcome. I don't know if it was Elsie's medicine or spending so long in the darkness of the forest, but the island, laid out far below us surrounded by a glistening sea, took my breath away.

"Is that the village in the harbour?" I asked, pointing far off. "And the little boats tied up?"

"It is!" replied Quentin. "I can see the line of cottages, and over there, that's Dead Man's Cove! And look at that wonderful old boat, it looks significant. I wonder who sails it."

Squinting, I saw it too- anchored far below, a beautiful schooner at half-mast. "It all looks unreal, like a perfect toy," I gasped as I looked down in wonder.

"Now I know how the Greek gods felt," replied Quentin. "And it really does feel nice, peering down on it all from a height. Say, is that Rookscroft?"

I strained to see, and behind the village, high up on the hill, I could make out the house, its windows glinting in the afternoon sun.

"It is," I cried. "I can see our home!"

"If we had a good telescope, we might even be able to peek in through the windows," said Quentin (he was talking quickly and with much excitement). "I could see right into the library from here, the fireplace, Robin's book still open where we left it. Say, is that smoke coming from the chimney?"

My heart leapt. Perhaps Robin had made it home, though I had no idea how he could have lit the fire, but it was just an errant cloud drifting near the chimney.

"I just want to be back there," I sighed. "I'm so tired, Quentin. If only I could grow a pair of wings and drift back down."

"You might need to grow them, Miss, but I already have mine," he said. "From here, I can easily take to the air. There's plenty of room for a take-off and landing." (He was considering the field as he spoke.) "I think it's an interesting idea, but we should stick together," I replied.

"If we just retrace our steps back to the fork in the path, we can take the right one down..."

"Climb all the way back up those rocks?" asked Quentin. "And perhaps even then we might get lost, and it's late in the day. It will take five minutes at most for me to check for sure, and you won't lose sight of me, I promise."

"I don't think it's a good idea," I said, remembering Elsie's warning "we should stick together."

"I promise not to leave the field, just a quick jaunt up to get our bearings." He replied.

"I'm really not sure, remember the owl." I said.

"Oh he's long gone by now" Quentin replied flippantly "and besides, just think, this could save us from climbing back up there, I'm sure he's still lurking about in the trees."

"Do you think you could scout things out without going very far?" I asked.

"Of course," he replied excitedly. "I'm up for a little aerial reconnaissance. It's been a while since I've flown, but it seems like a good day for it. If I can get above the treetops, I think I can spot the waterfall."

"That would be useful," I agreed, "but I'm worried about you flying. Please don't take offence, but you seem like more of the ground bird type to me."

"Technically you're right, but I'm only planning on making a quick loop of the clearing so we can get our bearings... Oh, this is exciting! I quite fancy myself as an aviator. I might need a new style of hat for my birthday."

"Speaking of hats, if you insist on going, perhaps you should leave yours with me," I suggested.

"Good idea," he replied.

His attention was on a large log to our left. "I think that's the one," he said, pointing with his wing.

I was gripped by a growing apprehension. "Quentin, you don't seem quite yourself," I said. "I really think you should stay on the ground. The more I think about it, the more I don't feel you're cut out for flying."

He wasn't listening and raised his wing in the air. "Wind coming from the south, slight breeze, should be no problem... I sound like Robin, all this talk of weather..."

He lifted his left leg and, tipping his head forward, removed his hat. "Hold onto this for me. I'll be back momentarily," he said. I noticed his eyes; they were shining and distant. Without his hat, he did not resemble my friend at all, but a wild bird, beautiful and strange.

"If I don't come back, remember me fondly," he called as he hopped down, emerging a moment later on the far end of the log he had selected. "This is such an adventure, Jayne. I feel like a real hero now, the kind you read about in books. Robin will be thrilled when he hears about this!"

He faced forward, looked up toward the sky, and crouched slightly. "I'll be back in a flash," he cried. He opened his wings and began to run forward, bringing them down then raising them again, and suddenly he was airborne.

It was a rather ungainly sight that seemed to break every rule of physics. His body hung low as he tucked in his feet, and I was sure he would not get far. A moment later he was halfway across the field and my heart was in my mouth as I watched him bank to the left. He turned and flew back, low over my head.

"I'm already quite tired!" he shouted. "But I have one more pass in me."

Quentin Taking to the Sky

He flew in a wide curve to the far side of the clearing, he appeared to look down then his head jerked back up-he had spotted something! He turned in an arc and began his return, his wings flapping wildly, long tail flowing behind. I felt so proud of him as he approached... and then I heard the wind.

It rumbled down behind me, through the bending trees, and blew past, beating at my back and pulling at my hair as it went by.

"Quentin!" I shouted, and the gust carried the word away as it raced across the field. I saw him brace as the fierce wind caught him, and I gasped in horror as he tumbled through the sky, higher and higher, farther and farther, over the treetops and out of sight.

My eyes searched the clouds, I tried to shout, but no sound came. I stood, fists clenched, my eyes fixed to the distance as I fell to my knees.

My mind could not comprehend that I had lost him and I began to cry. I don't know how long I was there, but slowly, I became aware of my body sobbing in that primeval way and as it subsided, I found myself crying "No" over and over as I scoured the dull heavens but he was gone.

I closed my eyes, rocked forward and backward. "No, please no, please, please not my friend, please help me," I prayed. I had never felt so alone.

Chapter Six

Puhpowee

The sound of pulsing whooshing air grew closer until it stopped above my head. A clatter of wings, a moment of silence, then a deep, croaky voice cried, "Why, why, why."

Squinting through my tears, I saw a large raven perched very near. It looked down, considering me, with its head tipped to the side, examining me with its shining eye, and as I watched, its large beak opened. "Why," it cried, "why, why."

"Please leave me alone," I said.

"Why, why, why," came its reply.

"Because I'm heartbroken," I sobbed, though I knew that seemed silly to say.

"Why, why, why," it croaked again.

"Because my friend was blown away, and I don't know what to do."

"Why, why, why."

"Please leave me alone. I know you don't understand."

"Why, why, why?"

"Oh, for goodness' sake." I pulled myself up to my feet and picked up my rucksack. "I'll leave you alone. This is probably your clearing and I'm sorry I bothered you."

Looking to the left, I spotted the wool I had tied to the trees. "Goodbye," I said, and I turned to go.

I had made my way over the first log when a new word reached my ears.

"Why, why, here?"

I turned and looked back at the raven, who was gazing at me expectantly.

"Did you just talk?" I asked.

"I've been talking all along, all along," replied the raven.

"I'm here because I'm lost," I said, "and I don't even know where 'here' is. I belong down there," and I pointed off in the direction of home.

"You're lost, lost, lost?" asked the raven in its low and cracking voice.

"Well, I don't know how it happened exactly," I replied. "I think someone has been messing with the wool."

The raven squinted; it looked confused. "Why, why, why?" it asked.

"The wool?" I said. "Well, Auntie Winnie gave it to us, and by us I mean Quentin and I, and now he's gone and..." I choked back a tear. "He went flying off over there." I pointed out over the trees. "The wind caught him and carried him off."

The raven hopped down next to me. It was spectacular to see, iridescent and as dark as coal. Its curved beak was fringed with feathers, and its eyes were inky black. I could not tell what it was thinking. Had I been foolish to mention Quentin? Might it set off to harm him? I had heard that crofters in Scotland feared ravens as they kill sheep, and I suspected they could make short work of a pheasant, especially one built for poetical musings.

"Why are you here, why here?" asked the raven again.

Where had my adventure begun? Each step had led to the next, which had brought me to this spot, though why I was there was difficult to say.

"I don't honestly know," I said, and the wind left my sails.

I slumped down onto the log and stared at the moss. The forest was still, save for the soft rustling of a breeze in the trees, and I felt numb; just a body, in a clearing, in a forest, and nothing more.

The raven kept his steady gaze.

I cannot say how long I sat there, but slowly my thoughts returned. An ant walked over my hand, and I brushed it away, then the call of a woodpecker in the distance. I looked up and watched as a weak shadow raced across the sky.

"Welcome back, you're back," said the raven.

Quentin was my first clear thought, my second Robin, and my eyes began to fill with tears again. What was I doing wasting time when they were in such danger? "Can you help me find my friends?" I asked.

A Raven in the Clearing

"Perhaps, I can, I can," replied the raven.

"Please, one of them is lost, but I believe he's safe. The other... I am SO afraid for him."

"Where did he go, he go?" it asked, and I pointed to the tall trees where I had last seen him. It followed my finger with its eye, then turned to me and tilted its head-perhaps it was thinking.

"Yes," I said. "Is that bad?"

"Out to sea, the sea," it replied and nodded its head. Then, leaning forward, it opened its vast black wings and took to the sky. I watched as it flew away, over the treetops and out of sight.

Time passed in the quiet forest and I felt empty and sad, so I climbed the tallest stump to look down on my home again, but now there was no view. Low clouds had rolled in from the sea, obscuring the world below, and I felt utterly alone.

The air grew cold, and my feet went numb. I reached into my rucksack to take out the blanket, and Quentin's hat tumbled out. I picked it up, it was so small and worn, and the inside rim was shiny where it had rested on his precious head. I drew the thick blanket around my shoulders and sat on a tree stump, holding it in my hands like a prayer.

It felt like forever, and I began to think the raven had left for good. A foggy cloud was creeping through the trees below, I watched as it advanced, obscuring the trunks in its thick, cold veil. It began to move towards me over the field and I was not sure where to go. I could see the red wool tied to the tree; it had not reached there yet and I thought if I left I could make my way down to it, I could leave and if I was lucky and took the right turn, I would be back with Elsie before it was dark.

What had she said about Quentin? That his future was uncertain, that she could not tell if he would meet Robin again. She must have seen it in the leaves. It was Quentin who had been in danger all along. I realised that now. I was the one entrusted to protect him, and I had let him go.

I tucked his hat into my pocket, grabbed my rucksack, and quickly walked down the field towards the trail, Elsie was my only hope. It was cold as I entered the fringes of the fog. My foot slipped on the damp moss and twisted as it landed between two stones. I stopped and waited for the pain, but after a moment, there was nothing, and I thanked the stars and continued on. The fog was all around me now, cold and swirling as the trees began to fade from view. I had made a mistake.

"Up here, here," came a cry. "Up here, here."

I saw the dark raven circling above my head. "This

way, the way, this way" it called, and slowly it began to drift uphill. I turned and followed it, up out of the fog, to the very top of the clearing where it landed on a branch and waited.

"Did you find him?" I called out as I approached.

"He's in the clouds, the clouds," replied the raven. "In the clouds, the clouds."

My heart lurched in my chest, what could he mean? I was cold, but I no longer cared. "I have to go and find him, he's my responsibility." I said. "Thank you for trying to help, but I can't just stay here when he is lost."

"So are you, are you," replied the raven, looking at me with its shining eye.

"But he's lost and in danger," I replied.

"So are you, are you," replied the raven.

It was right.

"All this talking is not going to find him," I said impulsively. "Thank you for your time," and I turned to head back down towards the trail, but I saw, to my dismay, that it was almost dark. I had no oil left in my lamp; there was nothing more I could do.

"You may die in the woods, the woods," said the raven. "I will take you to safety, to safety...I will take you to Puhpowee, Puhpowee."

"Puhpowee?" I struggled to pronounce the word. "Who is he?"

"You will see, you'll see, follow me," replied the raven. "Night is falling, it's falling..." With wings outstretched it swooped to the ground between the trunks of two great trees, "Follow closely, closely, follow me" it cried, as it turned and walked off into the forest with long, swaggering strides.

I trotted to catch up then followed close behind, I was out of breath and struggled to keep pace as we ascended through the dense trees. It was dark now, and the forest closed around us as the path began to narrow. I could barely see my feet; I could barely see the raven. The only sound I could hear were its faint footsteps on the trail.

"Where are we going?" I called out.

It did not reply.

"I can't go on," I cried. "I can't see a thing; I just can't walk into nothing."

I stopped. It must have stopped too; the world was quiet and still. I could not see. I blinked my eyes, but open or closed, my view was the same-utter blackness.

"Are you still there?" I asked.

"Puhpowee, Puhpowee, bring us light, light," squawked the raven.

A pale green glow appeared, so faint at first I thought my mind was playing a trick, but slowly it grew brighter and spread, illuminating both sides of the trail. Nature revealed her magic as a thousand tiny mushrooms lit our way.

"Thank you, thank you," squawked the raven, and it continued on with confident strides.

I followed just a step behind, captivated by the scene and I wished my friends were by my side so they could see it too. Above us tree branches knitted together, obscuring the blue black sky, and slowly the path transformed into a tunnel, which gradually became smaller. I had to crouch as I made my way along and bowing my head, I saw the mushrooms more closely and their translucent caps reminded me of jellyfish I had once seen in the bay.

Glowing Mushrooms Lead the Way

The tunnel ended suddenly and I stepped into a round forest room, its walls were towering pines that reached into a star-filled sky. At its centre, a bright fire burned, and sitting on the far side, warm eyes smiling down upon us, sat the great spirit Puhpowee.

He was incarnated as a wolf who sat upright but at ease on a throne of a velvet green that matched his smiling eyes. About his shoulders, he wore a cloak fashioned from cedar bark adorned with shells. "Welcome to my woods," he said, and his straight white teeth and glistening tongue flashed in the firelight.

I was afraid.

"Come forward, child," he instructed as he beckoned me over with his huge grey paw. I made my way to him and stood at his feet. I did not see the raven anymore. The flames crackled behind me. I no longer saw the forest. I no longer saw the sky. There was only Puhpowee leaning in toward me with an amused smile.

Up close, he was large and imposing, his eyes looked deeply into mine.

The Wolf and the Raven

"What brings you here?" he asked. "This is no place for a human."

"My friends are lost," I answered, and the journey played like a movie in my mind.

Puhpowee nodded. He had seen it too.

"I have no special gifts regarding the sky," he said thoughtfully, "but perhaps I can help you with your friend in the ground. First, let me attend to you, my guest. You are cold and tired, here, have some broth."

He handed me a wooden bowl. It looked so small in his great paws, but when I took it from him, it was large and heavy in my hands. The broth was warm and tasted of the earth.

"It will do you good," said Puhpowee, nodding to himself.

When I was done, he took the empty bowl, slowly wiped it clean, and placed it by him on a ledge.

Puhpowee

"Now let us see if the mushrooms can help you find your friend," he said. "They know the forest's secrets." He slowly rose from his seat, and towering over me, looked into my eyes down the length of his handsome nose and seemed to smile.

"This way," he said, and I followed him around the fire, where the earth had been drawn away to form a shallow pit. It was lined with lichen and soft moss. The word grave flickered through my mind-was this the end? It did not feel so bad.

"Lie down and rest," instructed the wolf. "Make yourself comfortable; this is your cradle in the earth."

I sat on the warm ground, then lowered myself in and lay on my back on the soft padded hole.

The warm fire crackled beside me as I looked up into the heavens. The moss and the lichen smelled fresh and alive. The wolf took a seat by my side and placed his great paw on my head. "Not up there," he said kindly. "Close your eyes and feel the life beneath you, deep within the ground."

I did as he instructed, and in my mind's eye, I saw a web of white, intricate and lacy under my body, spreading out to every side.

"That's it," said the wolf, reading my thoughts. "Now

follow it out and see the world from the mushrooms' view. They connect us all. Think of where you would like to be."

Rookscroft came into my mind, and in an instant, I was flying along a glowing tube, smooth and fast as it raced down the mountain, then effortlessly rose on the other side, along a path that wound and curved. "This must be the lane," I whispered. I paused at the gate, then hopped from patch to patch across the field and through the orchard until I reached a large gnarled tree where I travelled up and came to rest on the side of the trunk.

"Open your eyes and see," said the wolf.

I was back at the house! Viewing it from the large conch that grows on the oak tree by the study window. A warm light glowed inside the room.

"I always keep a light on," I whispered. "Perhaps Robin made it home."

"I do not see him here," replied the wolf. "Come, you must leave and search for him elsewhere."

I glanced back at the house. It seemed so close and real. I could see the wallpaper on the far side of the room and the paintings I had hung, and there on the table, a book lay open-the book we had been reading before we left. I could even make out the sea beast on the page.

"Little Robin," I gasped, remembering how he had jumped in distress when he first saw it.

"Let us find him now," came the wolf's deep voice, and the house was gone. I closed my eyes, and I was back underground, effortlessly flying along in a vast web of white, first jumping from spot to spot back over the fields and then, skipping the lane altogether. We were in the forest now, and the web became brighter and flickered with life. Up and down, to the left and right, we travelled underground. I was moving at such speed that for a moment I felt unwell but Puhpowee touched my forehead, and the movement slowed. Now we were moving an inch at a time, further into the earth, down an intricate tunnel of soft white filament, and a moment later we were there.

"Is this Robin?" asked the wolf. I opened my eyes, and saw my beautiful friend, tucked up in a neat little bed, sleeping soundly. The tiny room was clean and cosy, its walls and floor were polished earth, and a single candle flickered on a table by the door.

"Where is this?" I asked, and as I watched, the door slowly opened, and a small round mole poked in his head.

"Looks like he's gone off to visit the land of nod," he said.

"That's good, Grenville. Now come out quickly before you wake him again. Would you like more supper?"

"That depends if you have more of those nice little pies, and I wouldn't mind a drop of sherry," the mole replied, and he turned and left the room, quietly closing the door behind him.

I sat bolt upright and turned to look into Puhpowee's smiling eyes.

"I saw him," I said.

"You did," replied Puhpowee. "Would you like me to take you to him?"

"Yes please" I cried "Can we also look for Quentin?"

"Place your hand in mine," instructed the wolf. His paw was huge and the pad rough. He closed his eyes and began to chant softly.

I closed my eyes and behind the lids I saw soft colours dance.

"Your friend is not on the land," he said finally. "I am sorry, but do not lose hope. First, let us go to Robin."

I eased onto my feet, excitement, sadness, hope and fear were mixed together in my mind. I saw the raven; it had been watching from a nearby tree.

"Sacha, will you join us?" asked the wolf, and it glided down and landed on his left shoulder.

Together we set off to find dear little Robin and as I walked I felt so small beside my new friend-he was magnificent and strong, yet he moved with an air of lightness and presence that comforted me.

Our journey took us through dense forest, where we had to walk single file as we followed the narrow trail. I kept my eye on Puhpowee's back, he traveled quickly with long strides and I struggled to keep up. The path ahead was lit by mushrooms, but after we had passed, they quickly faded, leaving a curtain of darkness that followed just just steps behind.

We seemed to walk all night. I thought I saw dawn break far off, beyond the trees.

"Morning is approaching, and we are almost there," said Puhpowee as if reading my thoughts. "Come, this way. Just a little further, and here, take this." He stopped, reached into his cloak, and handed me a bag made of muslin tied with twine. "Make a hot broth with this," he instructed. "It will sustain you and help you on your journey." I took the bag gratefully and thanked him.

We were standing in a small clearing, and in the early

morning light, I saw a dark line of water emerging from the trees; a babbling stream with a bank on one side that ran by the side of a trail. Together, we walked to its mossy edge.

"Take some," said the wolf. "It is safe to drink."

Sacha hopped from his shoulder and landed on the bank. He submerged his black beak, then flung back his handsome head and took a drink. I knelt down beside him and cupped my hands, and immersed them in the dark, clear stream, then brought them up to my mouth. The water tasted sweet and good. I dipped them in again and lowered my face to the freezing water. It filled my nose and kissed my eyes, baptising me for the new day.

"Guide her home," the voice behind me said, and when I turned to see, Puhpowee had faded away, leaving Sacha and me alone by the water's edge.

"Where did he go?" I asked.

"Home, home, he's home," replied Sacha.

"Without saying goodbye?" I asked.

"Why, why, why?" asked Sacha.

And I could not answer because whatever I knew he knew too, so I said goodbye and thanked him with my heart.

I noticed the trail of mushrooms that ran along by the side of the stream and, at the bend, they curled up a mossy bank and ended by a door. It was about the size of my hand, round and painted the colour of a hazelnut shell. I got to my feet and quickly made my way over and knelt down before it on the path. The little brass knocker was at eye level. I reached up, lifted it with the tips of my fingers, and rapped it several times.

"Who can it be at this hour?" came a voice from behind the door.

"Well, go on, answer it. We shan't know who it is until you answer," came the reply.

"All right, let me get the lamp lit."

"Well, hurry up, or they may be gone."

"That might be a good thing. Goodness only knows who's prowling about out at this early hour."

The door opened slightly, and a slender velvet nose poked through the crack and began to sniff the air.

"Is it someone we know, Grenville?"

"Give over, how would I know? I haven't seen them

yet..." Grenville replied.

The door opened a little further, and I could see a very fine mole dressed in a nightgown, wearing silver-rimmed spectacles near the end of his nose. His eyes were little twinkles in his fur and he leaned toward my face, brandishing a lamp.

"Yes?" he asked in a small yet commanding voice.

"Hello," I said. "I'm looking for a friend."

"Who is it?" called a second voice from deep inside the home.

"Well, how would I know that, Ivy? They haven't told me yet," said Grenville. "They're looking for a friend."

"Aren't we all," replied Ivy.

"I'm sorry," I said. "My name is Jayne, and I'm looking for my friend Robin."

Mr & Mrs Mole at Their Door

"Robin? You mean a robin bird?" asked Grenville, peering up at me through the gloom.

"Yes, that's right," I replied. "My friend Robin. He's a bird."

"Well, we don't have robins round here," answered Grenville, removing his spectacles and cleaning them carefully on the corner of his nightgown. "Now, it's my understanding that robins are more of a garden bird. They favour worms, and I can't say I blame 'em."

"I'm sorry," I said. "I don't think I made myself clear. I'm looking for my friend, and his name is Robin, but he's not a robin, though he is a bird. He calls himself a dip quail; half button, half California. My friend Puhpowee told me he was here."

"Well, that's confusing," replied Grenville, replacing his spectacles and peering up at me with his tiny pinprick eyes.

"Honestly, Grenville, get out of the way." Ivy appeared to his left and nudged him to the side. She was a small water vole with very pretty eyes.

"I heard you say you're looking for a friend, a bird... Is his name, by chance, Robin?" she asked.

"YES!" I said. "YES, have you seen him?"

"Seen him? Why, he's dozing in our kitchen in an armchair by the fire!" she replied jubilantly.

"I didn't know you knew Robin," said Grenville excitedly. "Why didn't you say so? All this nonsense about buttons! Come in, come in!"

He stepped aside, and I could see a small passageway curving off behind him, its polished floor lit warmly by candlelight.

"I'm afraid that won't be possible," I replied. "I think I'm a bit too tall."

Grenville looked at me in shock.

"Well, I simply don't understand," he said, taking a step forward and reaching out toward the bridge of my nose. "You look to be the same height as me."

"That's my nose," I replied. "See, my eyes are on either side."

He swung his tiny lantern left and right, and a look of horror crossed his face. "Good lord, what are you? Some kind of giant?" he gasped.

"I'm a person," I replied.

"A person?" whispered poor Grenville leaning forward

with the lantern. "Well, I never. I suppose you'd better wait here, then, while I fetch him." And with that, he turned and slowly shuffled back into the house.

"It's an awful shame you can't come in," said Ivy. "We just redid the parlour, and I've been wanting to show it off to a visitor such as yourself. Lovely it is. Grenville did such a fine job with the plastering."

"Your home does look so charming, from what I can see," I replied. "It's just so lovely and cosy."

"Cosy?" cried Ivy. "I hope you are not trying to imply our house is small. This is a fine residence, the finest on the bank, fit for a king it is..."

"I'm sorry," I replied. "I hope I didn't offend you. I just meant that it looks so warm and friendly, that little passageway behind you lit by candlelight."

"There you go again with the little," said Ivy indignantly. "I'll have you know that the hallway is the grandest in the area! Now, if you'll excuse me, I'll go and see what my husband's up to." And with that, she turned and shuffled out of sight.

While I waited for their return, I looked around. Above me, the dark blue sky was tinged a milky white toward the east. A new day was here. I felt chilled, and a wave of exhaustion swept over me as I kneeled on the cold, mossy ground.

There was movement at the end of the hallway, shadows on the walls, muffled talking. I leaned forward and watched as three little creatures made their way to the door. I heard Robin's voice, and a moment later he was standing right before me, his large eyes shining as he struggled to see out into the dark morning. My heart leapt, and I began to cry.

"Jayne, is that really you?" he asked.

"Yes, my friend," I replied. "Oh, Robin, I'm so happy to have found you! Here..." I extended my left hand, palm up, so that he could hop on, and I felt the familiar tickle of his fine claws on my fingers as he steadied himself.

"Found me?" he asked, looking up toward my face. "Was I lost? But I thought I had lost you." He blinked heavily and began to look around. "Where's Quentin? Is he sleeping in the bag? If you can just pop me in there, please, after I say goodbye. The fireside was nice, but it's not the same as tucking under his wing."

He turned to his friends who stood together at the door. "Thank you for looking after me," he said. "Only now I've found my family, so I'll be heading home. You should visit us too; our house is big like yours. It's over the hills, away from the forest. If you follow the path, it will take you there. We have a nice library with books about mythical beasts, including sea monsters, and if you do come, you can share our bedroom too. But now I have to go. Quentin must be sleeping in the bag, and I would like to join him for a nap because he is very nice and warm to sleep by. The feathers under his wing are the softest, but he doesn't always let me go there because he says it tickles, but sometimes he does. Oh, and thank you again, and thank you for the cake. It was very delicious, Mrs Mole."

"Well, you're welcome, Robin," replied Ivy warmly. "Would you like to take a slice with you? I wrapped it up specially." She held out her little hand and extended a package.

"Thank you kindly," replied Robin as he took the tiny parcel with his beak and placed it in my palm. "There looks to be plenty here. I can't wait to share it with Quentin and Jayne."

Ivy glanced toward me disapprovingly. "Be sure to take plenty for yourself," she said. "Some people are gannets."

"Gannets?" said Robin. "No, this is Jayne, and she is not a bird. And Quentin, well, Quentin is a golden pheasant. Would you like to meet him?"

"Don't wake him on our account," said Grenville. "It's still very early. Mrs Mole means that some people are greedy as gannets, and I can tell you, I had an uncle who once visited the coast, and those birds can't half eat."

"Oh," replied Robin blankly. "Well, I've never been to the coast. Is that near the sea? I don't want to meet any sea monsters. I hear they eat ships."

"I think it's time to go," I suggested softly. "We could all do with a little more sleep before the sun is properly up. Let me slip you in my pocket, where it's nice and warm."

"But the bag?" asked Robin. "Where's the bag? And Quentin?"

"Come, say goodbye to your friends, and I will tell you all about it on our way back to the lodge," I replied, trying to hide the catch in my voice. "Don't worry, everything will work out. Remember, we are on a grand adventure."

"Oh yes!" replied Robin. "This is a fun game! Is he hiding? How I love it when we play hide and seek."

"In a manner, yes," I said.

"Hide and seek!" cried Grenville from the door. "Well, I haven't played that since I was a lad. You're going to have a fine day of fun, my young friend. Oh, and one last thing..." he had pulled something along the hall behind him, so large that it almost obscured the light. "Take this,"

He stood to one side so that I could carefully retrieve it from the doorway, a little package wrapped in muslin that I slipped into my pocket.

Robin waved and didn't complain as I carefully tucked him down into the bottom of my coat pocket before making my way back onto the path.

"Home now, home, home," called Sacha as we approached.

"Yes, please. Can you help us find the lodge?" I asked.

"The falls, the falls, the falls," replied Sacha.

"Yes, the falls will be perfect," I replied.

We retraced our steps along the narrow trail that ran beside the stream and Robin settled down to rest, I gingerly touched the soft feathers on his back with the tips of my fingers, and I felt him sigh as he drifted off to sleep.

I followed Sacha back into the dense moss covered trees, the path narrowed and grew darker as the branches overhead knitted together into a dense green canopy above. Without Sacha's help, I could never have found my way back.

We made our way in silence. I was so tired that

dreams began to form before my eyes and blend in with the scenery. I wasn't sure what was real anymore, and I steadied my mind by focusing on the sound of my footsteps as I walked along the trail.

Was that Quentin? I saw him in the branches of a tree, stretching up to meet the morning light but as I watched, his body became a patch of lichen and his tail a fern frond that quivered in the morning breeze.

My heart dropped and then I remembered Robin and I slipped my fingers into my pocket and lightly touched his dear little head, he was my comfort and hope on this cold endless day. I walked. Time faded. My legs ached ... I heard a sound that shook the air-a distant noise, deep and trembling, that grew steadily louder with each step. The path ahead curved to the right, and as we rounded the bend, we were standing in a veil of mist that rose up to the sky, and beyond it, a thundering curtain of water plummeted from the clouds.

We were back at the base of the falls! Sacha stopped and turned towards me "I must go, now go" he said.

"Oh of course, thank you so much my friend" I replied "We would have been lost without you, how can I ever repay you for your kindness?"

"No need, no need, no need" he squawked and bowed his head. He turned toward the falls. and took to the air, gliding effortlessly over the plunging pool and landing on the stone abutment of the bridge where he called his name three times into the sky.

From every direction, his friends replied, a cacophony of ravens calling back. A rhythmic beating of wings, and three great ravens descended from the mist, circling above him. He glanced over as if to say goodbye then glided up to join them and I watched as they slowly curled out of view.

The familiar path felt comforting, and the brightening morning felt like a new beginning. I dearly felt the urge to turn left and follow the cobbled lane home to Rookscroft. Perhaps Quentin would be waiting in the kitchen, and we could share the story of our adventure as we sat beside the fire. We were only a couple of hours from home and we could sleep in our own beds tonight! But sense got the better of me and I decided first to go back and check at the lodge. It was just along the lane, he might be there waiting for us,

With a spark of hope glowing in my heart, I crossed the bridge, and trotted down the path to the lodge. My heart skipped when I saw it, so pretty and serene between the trees. It seemed only yesterday that we had arrived; surely today we might all go home together.

Perhaps Quentin is inside! I reached the door and glanced down as I leaned in to push it open. On a cushion of moss that grew against the house, I saw a little crop of toadstools and Puhpowee's words flashed through my mind: "Your friend is not on the land," and my heart sank, for that meant he was truly lost.

Chapter Seven

The Sky and the Stars

I opened the door with no pleasure or excitement. The room was just as we had left it, and it broke my heart to see the note that Quentin had placed on the table for Robin. I made a fire, and once it was going, I sat on the sofa and ate a chunk of cake washed down with icy water from the pump. The room began to warm and I curled up on the sofa, around the pocket in which Robin slept, pulled the blanket up over my head, and fell asleep.

My dreams were black and mysterious. Serpents rose from an inky sea and curled their way into the dark night sky, transforming into black birds as they flew towards the stars. A sliver of a crescent moon hung above a caravan, which swooned and lifted into the snow-filled air, drifting off over an endless ocean towards the jagged mountains. But nowhere, even in my wild dreaming, did I see my precious friend.

I was woken by Robin's dear little voice. "Excuse me, Jayne, but isn't it almost supper time?" he asked.

I opened my eyes to the dim light of evening. The room was in shadow, and the embers of the fire glowed red in the hearth. Little Robin stood on the blanket just inches from my face, regarding me, hopefully.

"Supper time, yes," I said brightly. "That's a wonderful idea. Let me feed the fire and see what I can find."

"When will Quentin be joining us?" asked Robin, "only I really am missing him right now."

"So am I," I replied.

I carefully peeled back the blanket and made my way over to the fire.

"Is he on an adventure?" asked Robin.

My back was to him as I stoked the fire, so he did not see my face as I struggled to reply.

"An adventure, yes, in a way, I suppose," I said finally. "But Robin, I'm not sure where he is. He got lost, and we need to find him. Can you help me?"

"Like hide and seek?" asked Robin earnestly. "Oh, Yes! He likes to hide behind the curtain in the bedroom and pop out to scare me; that always makes me laugh. Perhaps he's there waiting for us, and if he is, won't he be very hungry by now? Or he might be down in the kitchen. I would like to go home now, please, so we can all be together."

I couldn't turn around and let him see my tears, and I let them fall onto the hearth while I gathered myself.

"Quentin isn't at the house right now." I said "I met a very wise wolf who could see many things, and he told me that Quentin is not on the ground of the island anymore."

"He'll be in the sky!" he replied brightly. "That's the answer-he is up in the sky!" And he hopped over to the window and looked out hopefully while I made my way to the kitchen.

I lit the lamp and took stock of our meagre provisions: the heel of a loaf, now quite dry; an apple; salted hazelnuts in a bag and a tin of loose tea.

"I didn't see him up there, and it's almost night." Called Robin from the window. "I hope he's landed somewhere safe," He hopped down, crossed the room, and fluttered up onto a chair. "Oh, I do wish we had some soup to dip that crust in," he said wistfully, looking at the bread.

I remembered the dried mushrooms in my pocket.

"Don't worry, little friend. I'm sure we'll find Quentin if we put our heads together," I replied. "You know, I might be able to make us some soup. Why don't you sit where it's warm, and I'll join you once I have the ingredients together."

"Soup!" cried Robin, and his eyes lit up. "That sounds lovely; I hope that wherever Quentin is, there is someone to make him soup too, though I think he'd prefer cake and a spot of tea... He thinks soup is a bit messy to eat and always says, 'Robin, avoid the soup if at all possible; it's a devil to get out of the feathers if you spill it.'" He captured Quentin's voice so well that I laughed.

I took the package from my pocket and unfolded it on the table. It contained a mix of dried mushrooms and fragrant herbs, which I tipped into a small iron pot, then added water and salt from the bottom of the hazelnut bag.

I had seen people cooking over an open fire before and remembered that they pulled the hot embers out and placed the pot directly onto them, so I did the same. Then, I sat on the floor and stirred the soup. As it came to a boil, the dried mushrooms rose to the surface and danced on the bubbling water, but after a while, they began to flesh out and slowly sank down as the soup began to thicken. A dancing curl of steam rose up and filled the room with a good earthy scent, and my mouth began to water.

After it had cooled, I ladled out the soup, dropped in the crusts, and set out our supper beside the fire.

Robin sat next to me on a cushion with his saucer. "Well, that does smell good-like the earth after a summer rain," he said.

"It does" I agreed "isn't this room lovely and quaint? I can just imagine old Fritzl here with his friends, drinking beer and telling tales after a good day adventuring in the forest, but I must say that the boar's head is a sad touch, don't you think?"

Robin looked up above the fire. "A boar?" he said. "I thought it was a monster. Look at those huge fangs-maybe a sea monster even. But I don't think they have fur; with them, it's more like fish scales, I think."

"This one above the fireplace is a wild boar," I explained. "They used to roam the forests a long time ago. I thought Fritzl kept them as pets but I never knew he hunted them. Look at his fine face; it seems grotesque to have his head hanging there."

"Oh, I don't know," replied Robin, looking up cautiously. "I've seen pictures of the sea monsters, and they ate ships! Imagine what their land cousins could do to a house. I think he's safer where he is."

"He has such a handsome face," I said, looking up at him, his glass eyes catching the flicker of the fire. "I hope he didn't suffer."

"He might have eaten a lot of people back then," cautioned Robin. "Maybe even a whole town, and a little bird like me-or even one as big as Quentin-would just be a midday snack."

"I think the soup is cool enough to eat," I suggested, taking a sip from the spoon.

Robin bent forward and dipped in his beak. "It tastes just like it smells," he said approvingly, and we both fell silent while we ate.

What happened next is difficult to explain, but I will do the best I can.

I felt a warm, sinking feeling, and my body grew heavy. I settled back into my chair and took a long, slow breath. I looked over at Robin, who had puffed up his feathers and settled down, almost asleep, yet his eyes were open.

The edges of my vision seemed to dim, and the shadows in the room turned from black to a warm chocolate brown. The fire crackled softly, and the flames seemed to slow, swaying gently above the logs, exuding warmth and safety.

All my worries and fears just melted away, and we floated in that warm space in front of the fire, with the feeling that nothing existed outside the room-just Robin and I and the fireplace and the boar. And then he spoke.

"Good evening, friends, and thank you for joining me."

He looked down from his place above the mantle, regarding us with his dark, sparkling eyes, and his mouth curled slightly in a kindly way.

"I heard your conversation. Thank you for the compliments, but please don't think ill of Fritz, I am Albrecht, his best friend. I died at a ripe old age, and it was entirely my own silly fault-you see, I choked on an acorn. He was very distressed at my death and built this little cabin over my favourite wallow and placed me here so I could share his company. We had wonderful times in the old days-the parties, the laughter, the beer! He's in the stars now, looking down, but he often visits, and we spend fine times together. I saw you enter, and I watched as you danced, little Robin. You have some fancy feet, my friend! And now you have returned, but I see you are missing one of your party-Mr Quentin if I remember correctly."

My eyes began to fill with tears, but the rest of my body sat warm and still, except for my heart, which made a queer twinge. A line of little teardrops ran down Robin's cheek as he looked up.

"He's lost," I said, "and we can't find him. He's not on the island, and we have no idea what to do."

"And he's not at home either," added Robin, "because a wolf said so."

The boar looked down with his warm brown eyes. "Your answer might lie in the skies," he said, and lifting his head, he looked up towards the ceiling, and the most extraordinary thing happened. The roof simply faded away, revealing the dark night sky sprinkled with stars.

"Wow," gasped Robin. "How did you make that happen? Oh, look! It's Ursa, the great bear."

"I'm not sure I see a bear," I confessed, "but the stars do look beautiful."

Albrecht

And suddenly, we were among them. Our bodies still sat by the fire, but our awareness soared above in the dark velvet night.

"See," said Robin, pointing over, "there is her back and her legs and her tail and her head. I like to think of those stars as her ears." And as he spoke, a fine line traced its way from one star to the next.

"I see her, Robin," I gasped as the lines formed her shape.

"She has a special trick, too," Robin said. "If you follow the line of that star on her back out for the length of five, then it points to the North Star, and you can use it to find your way. Ancient sailors did-it helped them navigate the mighty seas."

I looked over to the North Star that twinkled and shone a radiant white.

We seemed to be floating higher.

"Have you ever seen a wandering star?" asked Robin. "I have. They like to play tricks and dance in the sky. And there's the Milky Way."

A glowing line of pink that traced an arc across the sky.

"It's beautiful," I said.

We were floating in the heavens.

I heard Albrecht's voice in my head. "Let's find your friend," he said.

And suddenly, we were looking down over the earth. The moon cast its twinking silver light over the blackness of the seas, and far below, I saw our island taking form. Amber lights flickered in the harbour, and behind them, further up, sat Rookscroft on the hill. Across the bay, the thick forest of the Wild Woods clothed a great mountain capped with snow.

"Call out to him," instructed the boar, and every moment I had known him flashed before my eyes. In a blaze of golden wonder, I saw it all-every feeling, every joke, all the silly stories all together-and I knew that Robin saw them too. Our hearts called out to Quentin.

In an instant, we were there, hovering over a cove where a line of rocks ran out to sea. There were five in all, and on the very last one was Quentin. He was alive but very cold, his wings folded tightly about him and his head tucked down near the ground. I heard Robin call his name, and to my amazement, he looked up, and I heard him whisper, "Robin."

Then, SNAP, we were back by the fire.

"I saw him," stammered Robin. "I saw him, and I think he saw me too."

"I know he did," I said, reaching over and touching his soft head. "You brought him comfort, Robin; now he knows you're safe. And now we've seen him, and we know where he is; we can go and find him."

I looked up at the boar and saw that he had returned to his other form-a dusty head stuffed with straw-but I knew that he was watching over us, and my heart swelled with gratitude. I stood on tiptoe, kissed my fingers, and placed them on his leathery snout. "Thank you so much, my dear friend," I said. "You have given us great comfort tonight."

"Well, I'm glad he didn't turn out to be a sea monster, and it was nice of him to show us where Quentin is," said Robin as I sat back down. "Can we go and fetch him now, please? He did look very cold on that wet rock, and I think he'll be glad to see us."

"That rock is a long way off," I replied thoughtfully. "We need to wait till daylight and figure out a plan."

"But it didn't look very far away, really," replied Robin. "And when I said Quentin's name, he heard me, so it can't be that far at all."

I wasn't sure how to reply. I wasn't sure what had

happened myself.

"That was a special gift of magic seeing," I explained. "He is on the rock way out to sea, and that's a long way off. It's dark now, so why don't we get a little sleep, and in the morning, we'll go and find him together."

"Will we be there in time for breakfast?" asked Robin sincerely.

"We'll do our best," I replied. "But we don't have much to take."

The heavy swooning brought on by the soup came back in a soft, dark wave. I tucked my feet up on the sofa, and Robin hopped in next to me. I made a little nest for him with the blanket, then pulled the rest up under my chin and fell into a dreamless sleep.

Chapter Eight

The Judge

I woke to the dawn light that filtered through the window by the door and felt refreshed and eager for the day. Robin was already up; he was over by the record player, pushing on the arm.

"Do you think we can take this with us?" he asked. "The record, I mean. Only it did make Quentin laugh to see me dance."

"It made us both laugh," I said. "And yes, I'll put it in my rucksack, and we can take it home."

Robin fluffed up his feathers. "Oh, Jayne, can we go soon?" he asked, " Only I'm very excited to see Quentin again. I think it won't take long to get to him, and maybe we can be back home by lunchtime."

"First, we have to work out where he is," I said, as I reached into my rucksack to find a pencil and paper, "Hop on over, and perhaps between us, we can make up a map."

I loosely sketched the outline of the island as I remembered it-the village in the harbour, the house in the fields, the woodland and church on the far side, then I drew in the path that led to the Wild Woods and curved up and to the left over the bridge by the waterfall, and finally the lodge where we now sat.

"This is how I think it goes," I said once I was done. "What do you think?"

Robin looked closely at my work. "It's very good," he said after looking it over. "Is that the lodge where we are inside now? It's so small; how do we fit?"

"It's just a picture of the lodge," I reassured him, "like the pictures in the book in the library. They are drawings that represent real things, and they are not often to size."

"Ah, that makes sense," agreed Robin. "Or a book on elephants would be as big as the room, and it would be very hard to open the pages."

"Exactly," I agreed.

"Well, that's north," said Robin confidently, pointing

to the right side of the page, "because last night I saw the North Star, and if we were up in the air here, it was over there."

I drew a little compass on the map with the north pointing in the direction that Robin had suggested.

"Is that the sea?" asked Robin, pointing at the space around the island.

"Yes," I replied.

"Can you please draw a sea monster like on my maps at home so I can remember?"

I was about to begin when he interrupted, "Can you make it a bit farther off, please? Only we don't want to bump into it when we go to collect Quentin. Maybe you can put it on the far side-that's a long way for it to swim."

I sketched a sea monster, one of the old style, with a boar's head and tusks, and Robin nodded approvingly.

"Now, where do you think we saw Quentin?" I asked.

"Why, he was just here," replied Robin confidently, "On this side of the bay, on a rock, and I saw a cave nearby."

He pointed so specifically with the claw of his longest

toe that I did not question him for a moment, for as many things as he did not know, somehow, when he was sure, he was right. I drew in a little rock and, next to it, a cave.

"Can you draw Quentin and please make him happy?" he asked, "There were 5 rocks in all, and he was on the smallest one at the end. Can you add a little breakfast for him, too?"

He watched carefully as I sketched in the rocks, then Quentin and a slice of toast on a plate.

"That's good, but where's his hat?" asked Robin. "He wasn't wearing it when we saw him last night, and you've left it off too."

"That's because it's here," I explained, retrieving it from my bag. I held it out in my hand for Robin to see-it looked so small, so worn and personal, and I felt like crying again.

"Oh yes, there it is," replied Robin almost flippantly. "Please keep it safe; he'll need that to keep his head warm. It can be a bit windy by the sea. Speaking of which, I found something next to the sofa, Jayne. Can you tell me what it is?"

I looked down and spotted the neck warmer that Winnie had made for Quentin and leaned over to pick it up.

"When we were out looking for you, we met a very lovely beaver named Winnie, and she gave this to Quentin," I explained. "It kept his neck warm as we made our way home, but it was hard to get off, and I had to cut it a bit with a knife so he could get his head out."

"I see," replied Robin, inspecting it closely. "We should take it for him so he can wear it when we find him. If it was made with love, then he'll feel it, and I think that will make him happy."

"That's a fine idea," I replied, "and in the meanwhile, maybe you would like me to pop it into my pocket with you? It will make a nice little nest you can cosy up in; it does look a bit cold out."

"Thank you," replied Robin. "I would like that very much."

I gathered our things together and popped Robin into my coat pocket with the neck warmer, then glancing around one last time, I said goodbye to the boar and locked the door behind me as I left.

At the gate, I turned right, as Robin suggested, and began to walk along the path. "Does this look right?" I asked. "I'm not sure how far it goes, but everything looks very overgrown."

"I'm sure it's the right direction," replied Robin, "but I don't know how we'll get past all those trees."

Up ahead, the path faded to nothing as it neared the forest, and my heart sank. I wasn't sure what to do.

"We should call Sacha," suggested Robin and he looked up towards the pale grey sky. "Excuse me, Sacha, are you there, please?" he asked.

I wasn't expecting anything to happen; the forest was cold and still, then a raven called out from a tree nearby, then another, and another, and soon the sky was filled with their cries. Four black birds circled in the sky, and one of them descended and landed on a rock, just a few feet away.

"Sacha?" I asked.

"Sacha, yes. Sacha, Sacha," he replied.

"Oh, there you are," said Robin happily. "We're sorry to bother you again, but we thought you might be able to help us find Quentin."

"I saw you in the sky, the sky," Sacha replied.

"Yes, that was us!" Robin cried excitedly. "Were you there too? I didn't see you, but it was very dark-just like your feathers."

"We're trying to find our friend, and we saw him last night," I began.

"I saw him too, me too, me too," answered Sacha. "Come, I'll guide you, guide you."

He hopped down and began to walk into the trees; we followed close behind.

It felt strange going back into the forest-the last thing I had expected to do after being so close to home-and the melancholia that settled over my mind was hard to ignore. The boughs drew in overhead, and the familiar darkness returned as we wove our way around the ancient trunks of firs and cedars.

I had a nagging fear of getting lost again. If Sacha took off and left us, there would be no path to guide us back, so I kept my eyes fixed on him as he strode along and hurried to keep up. It felt like we walked for an age, but little by little, the forest began to change. The trunks became thinner, with more space between the trees. The ground changed too-dark soil, carpeted in pine needles, transitioned into sandy ground, dotted with stones and boulders dressed in pale green and yellow moss. We began to head downhill, leaving the forest behind, and emerged onto a wide open landscape, plains of yellow grass crisscrossed with fox trails. Above us, a barn owl drifted in the cloudy sky, and ahead lay the grey sea, calm and partially veiled in mist.

I walked to the edge of the cliff, where Sacha waited for us on a rock. It felt as though we had been travelling all day, but the weak disc of the sun that shone through the clouds indicated that it was around noon.

"You're here, you're here, here," said Sacha.

I looked out over the edge where a steep, narrow path cut into the rocks curved down into a bay. At the far side, past a beach piled with driftwood, the polished brass handle of a large round door glistened at the mouth of a cave.

"Down there, down there. Don't be shy, goodbye," croaked Sacha, and he turned toward the sea and dropped over the edge. I gasped as I leaned over, fearing I'd see him fall, but he shot past me on a wave of air and soared into the sky. "Sacha, Sacha, Sacha," he called. Three great ravens glided out of the thick trees each calling its own name and together they flew away over the wild, dark forest, leaving us all alone.

"I didn't get a chance to thank him," I sighed. "Let's go down to the bay."

"Yes, yes, let's," agreed Robin. "We'll pick up Quentin and go home and have tea. Maybe there's a boat down there-I hope there is-and someone to captain it, too. I'm a bit scared of bodies of water that are bigger than a bathtub."

"I understand," I answered kindly. "Well, I think the sea is a lot bigger than that, but at least it's not stormy today. You might want to tuck in my pocket while I climb down. I'm not the steadiest on my feet when heights are involved."

Robin wriggled down as I suggested, and I inched my way along the narrow steps, steadying myself by holding onto the grass that grew in thick tufts on the cliff beside me. It took a while to finally reach the beach, where delicate fans of orange-red seaweed formed a sweeping line where the ocean met the sand. Further back, lengths of glossy kelp with bulbs like living glass lay draped across the driftwood that rested by the rocks.

The sea lapped softly on the shore, caressing the sand with a fine line of foam. It was a peaceful place, but the fog that hung above the water lent a sense of foreboding.

The door was ahead of us, high up on a ledge, and from this angle, I could also see an ornate bowed window to its right. Below, great tree trunks, bleached white by the sea, lay piled against the rocks. It seemed that the only way up was to somehow climb over them and I was not sure what to do.

Robin popped his head out of my pocket and looked around. "Perhaps if we walk to the edge of the sea, we can see the rock where Quentin is waiting," he said.

"I don't think we can see anything out there today, not with all the fog," I replied, and he looked at me with such sad eyes that I instantly regretted my words. "But perhaps I'm wrong. Why don't we have a look? You never know, and if anyone can spot him, it's you."

I walked to the water's edge, where a wave rippled in and rolled over the ends of my boots, turning them dark and wetting my toes; it was icy cold.

Robin leaned forward and peered into the fog. "Look!" he cried. "I can see a rock!"

The veil of billowing clouds before us thinned, revealing a high grey rock that rose up from the sea.

"That's the first of them," cried Robin. "There are five in all, and they look like the bones in a tail, and Quentin is sitting at the very last one, just like you drew him on the map."

"Yes, he's at the very end," I replied, keeping my voice cheery as my heart was sinking. "The furthest out to sea. We're going to need help reaching him."

"Can't we just swim out and get him?" asked Robin. "I know how you like taking baths, and I once took a foot bath beside the fire, and in the summer, I like to dip my toes in the birdbath if it's not too deep."

"This is no bathtub, I'm afraid," I replied.

"Oh yes, of course, I forgot about the sea monsters," said Robin, looking around. "Do you think there are very many out there?"

"It's not the sea monsters that concern me," I explained. "It's very cold-too cold to survive a swim. If we are going to help him, we're going to need a boat."

I turned and looked back across the cove, from here I could see a wide stone staircase that led up from the sand.

"Do you think those steps might lead up to the big door?" Asked Robin.

"I think they might" I replied "let's go and see."

I made my way across the beach and climbed the curving stairs, they led to a wide stone shelf and there, as Robin had suggested, was the door. It was made from massive timbers, and the polished brass knocker was at its centre. I noticed the distinct but not unpleasant smell of fish, "What giant creature would live in this place with a door so wide and tall?" asked Robin. "You don't suppose it's a sea monster, do you? Who else would live in a cave home. Perhaps we should leave."

"Sacha brought us here, and I trust him." I replied, "And he wouldn't lead us into danger. I'm scared, too, but we have to find help if we want to rescue Quentin."

"I agree," whispered Robin. "I just hope we don't get eaten."

With some trepidation, I lifted the heavy knocker and brought it down three times, and the jarring smack echoed around the cove, sending a sandpiper whirling into the air with a queer, angry cry.

Silence.

The door was so large that I felt afraid, what creature would live in a place like this? I took a step back and was about to leave, but then I thought of Quentin out there all alone, whoever lived here might have a boat, and I hoped with all my heart that someone was home.

"Perhaps you should knock again," suggested Robin as he nervously peeked from my pocket.

We heard a noise from behind the door-a slow, heavy shuffling that grew steadily louder, accompanied by the smell of something fragrant and strangely familiar, and a voice, rich and slow, which said, "I'm almost there, hold on a moment, I'm almost there."

More shuffling, the sound of a handle turning, then the door slowly opened o n its heavy brass hinges, and before us stood a very majestic sea lion, wearing a paisley dressing gown and a purple velvet smoking cap embroidered with gold thread. He was shrouded in a cloud of smoke that emanated from a large and intricately carved tobacco pipe that he held aloft in his right flipper.

"Well, good morning to you," he said, looking down upon me with his kindly eyes and his mouth curled into a wide, toothy smile beneath his bristling whiskers.

"Hello," I replied. "Umm, I'm sorry to bother you, but a friend advised us to come here. He thought you might be able to help."

"Help?" replied the sea lion. "Well, of course. Do come in." He opened the door wide and stood to one side to let us pass.

The hallway was an enchanted grotto whose undulating shell covered walls were bathed in the light of a dozen flickering candles. The glow of soft pink opalescence invited us in..

Judge Dp Bonneville

He bowed as he passed us, then led us along the dream-like passage and into a round room, where the large bowed window we had seen from the beach looked out over the bay.

"That was taken from the captain's cabin of an old galleon," explained the Judge. "I especially appreciate the coat of arms."

Stepping forward, I saw that within the latticework of leaded glass, an intricate panel depicted a shield held aloft by a coiled sea serpent.

"That's very beautiful," I said. "I wonder who it belonged to."

"Well, I can tell you that," replied the sea lion jovially. "My name is D.P. Bonneville, by the way. Officially, I'm a judge, but you needn't mention that again if you don't want to. I only told you on the off chance that the help you are seeking is legal. I'm mostly retired now and spend most of my time here in the library with the company of my old books."

"Old books!" cried Robin, and he hopped out of the pocket onto my hand.

"Well, hello there little fellow," said the Judge. "And who might you be?"

"I'm Robin," said Robin excitedly, "and my favourite things are Quentin, cake, and books. I especially like the old ones."

"Well, I'm not sure who Quentin is, but you're bang on the money with your other likes," laughed the Judge, and his eyes sparkled.

"And this is Jayne," continued Robin, "and Quentin is lost."

"I'm sorry to hear that," replied the Judge. "And hello, Jayne," he smiled and slightly bowed his head.

"Now, Little Robin, if you like books, you're going to love this one-it's a cracker. Come over here and take a look." He beckoned us to follow as he went over to his desk and took a seat in a wide chair upholstered in tapestries. In front of him lay a wonderful leather-bound tome with etched brass plates that protected the corners. He placed his pipe in a wooden stand, then opened it with a careful turn of his flipper, revealing an illustrated page.

"Now step up, little fellow, and don't be shy. I bet you've never seen a book like this one before."

I lowered my hand to the table, and Robin hopped off and futtered over to the open page to take a closer look.

The Judge and Little Robin

"What is it about?" I asked.

"It's an account of the seas," replied the Judge, "written by the captain of the galleon named the San Juan El Mar. It ran aground in the cove here, heaven knows how long ago, and my forefathers preserved many of its treasures before the sea finally claimed it. To me, this was the greatest treasure of all. The window there is from the captain's cabin, too, just think he would have sat in front of it as he wrote this very book on the high seas."

"Did he happen to mention sea monsters?" asked Robin fearfully.

"Well, to tell you the truth, I haven't read the whole thing, but he may well have done. They used to believe in those sorts of things back then."

"I still do," whispered Robin, "but I don't think I want to see one close up."

"Me either," laughed the Judge. "There's enough in the water as it is without the added complications of sea monsters. Now, how can I help you? You mentioned a lost friend."

"Yes," I replied. "You know that line of rocks just off the cove?" I gestured out of the window. "Well, he's out on the little one right at the end, and we need to rescue him right away. Can you help us, please? Perhaps you know someone with a boat."

"How the devil did he get out there?" asked the Judge. "Why, no one in their right mind would go out there. The sea is as rough as all get out around those rocks, absolutely treacherous with the changing tides."

"He flew-or rather, the wind blew him, and he managed to land there," I explained.

"Well, rather there than in the sea, I suppose," replied the Judge, lifting his pipe and taking a puff. "But that's no place for a boat. It would get smashed to pieces on the rocks before it could even get near. Getting him off-now that's a real conundrum. Give me a moment to have a bit of a think."

He slowly rose from his chair and began to pace the room. "Mmm, and how long did you say he's been out there?" he asked.

"We didn't," I replied. "But he's been on the rocks for almost four days."

"Four days!" cried the Judge. "There's no shelter, and the winds are bitter. I'm afraid you might need to prepare for the worst."

"Does that mean he will be very cold?" asked Robin sincerely.

"Dead cold by my reckoning," replied the Judge. "Why, I don't know many who could live that long."

Robin looked around in a panic. "Does that mean?... " he began.

"If anyone can make it, it will be Quentin," I interjected, lowering my hand down next to him so he could hop back on. "Isn't that right, Robin?"

"Yes," replied Robin as he climbed onto my finger. "He's ever so strong. Sometimes, he lets me ride on his back if I trim my nails first so I don't scratch."

The Judge glanced over and, realising the sensitivity of the moment, smiled kindly. "Well, little fellow, if he's that strong, then I have no doubt he will be just fine. Now, I have just one last question: how big is your friend?"

"Why, he's very big indeed," replied Robin proudly, stretching out his wings to illustrate.

"He's a golden pheasant," I explained. "Big by Robin's standards but really not heavy at all. I often carry him about in a bag."

"Very good, very good," said the Judge, taking another puff of his pipe and nodding thoughtfully. "I don't go out very far these days, but I believe I can make it with the tide going out. If I wait up at the rocks until it turns, I can ride it back in. The only problem I see is that I can't get up on the rocks myself-they're much too steep-but if I can find Tom... He's generally about in the tide pools this time of day. I'm sure he can ride out with me. He's light and strong and lightning fast. He could scamper up and bring down Quentin with him if he's game for it."

"Thank you so much for helping..." I began, but the Judge raised a flipper.

"Don't thank me yet, dear. Wait until we're all safely back on land," he said.

"Well, I can thank you for trying, at least," I replied. "I know this won't be easy, and you were having such a nice day before we came."

"Nonsense," laughed the Judge. "There's nothing like a bit of an adventure! It's me who should be thanking you-it's been years since Tom and I went out together past the mouth of the cove. I'd best set out now while the tide's in our favour. Help yourself to food from the kitchen, make yourselves at home, and try not to worry. We should be back before dark."

He flashed a broad smile, showing a line of pointed teeth, then turned and hurried off along the passageway that led to the front door.

We went to the window and watched as he departed.

Despite his significant size, he moved gracefully as he made his way across the sand. He raised his head and turned to the left, waving a flipper in the air. An otter popped up from the tidepool and waved back. The Judge went over to join him, and they sat talking together as the Judge pointed out to ward the sea.

After some discussion, they made their way back across the beach and emerged at the top of the steps, near the door, where they removed their clothes and laid them carefully on the ground. We watched as they walked back over the sand to the edge of the water, slipped into a rolling wave, and were gone.

"I'm cold and hungry," said Robin. "Can we go to the kitchen and see if there is something warm to eat, please? Only my tummy's complaining, and I need nourishment to keep me sharp."

"Of course," I replied. "I think it's next door."

The kitchen was an empty cave. A small opening above the sink had been fitted with a window made from sea glass, and the weak blue light that filtered in gave the impression of being underwater. The table in the centre was fashioned from a block of weathered rock, topped with a panel of well-used driftwood, and on it lay a set of knives. In the corner, a low stone trough was filled with water and dark, curling seaweed.

Judge Bonneville & Tom Making a Plan

This was the kitchen of a sea lion-designed for a creature who dined on the bounty of the sea-but it offered no comfort for Robin and me.

"I hoped there might be a fire," sighed Robin.

"I'm afraid not," I replied. "He probably has no need for one."

"I don't think he makes cakes," said Robin sadly, "or drinks a nice cup of tea in the afternoon. What does he do for a treat?"

"We can ask him when he gets back, but I'll bet his treats are found in rockpools," I said. "I'm cold too, Robin. I think it might even be warmer outside. Shall we see?"

We made our way along the shell-lined passageway, opened the front door, and stepped outside. The wind had picked up, racing in from the sea, carrying sand that blew into my eyes.

"I think we should go back in," I said, and before Robin could reply, I stepped back into the hallway and closed the door.

In the living room, I turned the Judge's chair so it faced the sea. Taking a seat, I took the blanket from my rucksack and wrapped it around us.

"I don't suppose we have a bit of cake left?" asked Robin weakly. "I'm not feeling very well."

I felt around in my pocket and brought out the ball of waxed paper that had wrapped the cake. Unfolding it carefully, I found several crumbs, which I gathered into a little pile with my fingertips.

"Here you go," I said, holding them out in my hand, and he pecked at the crumbs hungrily until half were gone and then looked up.

"I would like to save the rest for Quentin," he said. "He's going to just love a nip of cake when he gets back, even if it's only half a beakful."

My stomach began to growl, and I remembered the apple in my bag. I fished it out, and polished it on the blanket until it shone, then took a large bite. It tasted of home, and I remembered that Frank picked it in the autumn, and I had kept it through the winter in a box on the pantry floor. It had been there when Quentin moved into the house and right next to him when we first met Robin. Now it was here, in my cold, stiff fingers, coming to the end of its journey in this sad, barren place. It seems silly to have sentimental thoughts about an apple, but that is where my mind led me, and I couldn't stop the tears.

"Is that a Cox's Orange Pippin?" asked Robin, eyeing it

curiously.

"Yes, I think it is," I replied, wiping my eyes. "Would you like a bite?"

"Yes, please," replied my little friend. I turned it toward him, and he pecked gratefully at the white flesh. "They're a favourite of mine," he said. "I love a nice nip of apple because my grandma once lived under a pippin tree, and she made the most lovely jams and jellies, and the taste reminds me of her."

"Perhaps when we're home, I could try making some?" I suggested. "I've never tried apple jam."

"It's a bit sweet, and there is cinnamon in it too, I think, because it tastes a bit like wood," he explained. "Do you think they will be back soon? It's getting late, and the sea monsters do tend to come out around dusk," he stared anxiously out of the window, "and Quentin likes to have afternoon tea at around four."

"Let's have a closer look," I suggested.

Robin hopped onto my hand, and I held him next to the glass. It didn't look promising outside; the wind had driven the mist from the darkening sky and whipped up whitecaps on the foreboding sea. The tide was almost in, and the great frothing waves had almost reached the driftwood.

"Oh dear," whispered Robin. "The wind is coming from the north. It's going to be a cold night."

I looked out toward the line of rocks that staggered out to sea and noticed a large dark form bobbing towards us on the tide with a small figure riding on the top.

"Look, Robin," I said. "Do you think that could be them?"

I watched as the shape made its way into the cove, carried closer in by each successive wave. As it drew near, I recognised Tom. He was sitting on what looked to be a rounded black boat, holding something to his chest. Closer, and I could make out a flipper paddling through the water-it was no boat but the Judge.

"They're here!" cried Robin, jumping up and down with joy.

For a moment, they disappeared behind a rolling wave, and then they were clearly in sight, heading for the steps-the Judge on his back, Tom sitting squarely on his large belly, feet straddled to each side, and in his arms a pile of pale, wet feathers with no distinguishable shape.

It did not look good.

"See, it's him!" cried Robin. "It's Quentin. I bet he's cold."

"Yes," I said. "It's very cold out there. Pop into my pocket and keep your head down until I tell you to come up."

Robin obliged without a word, and I tucked my gloves over him, put my blanket in the rucksack, and headed for the door.

I picked my friends' clothes up from the floor and carried them down the steps to the water's edge. The wind blew my hair across my face, and it was difficult to see.

"We are back," I heard the Judge shout. "My, that was quite the trip-here, take your friend..."

I crouched down and brushed the hair out of my eyes, and there was Tom. "He was alive when we found him," he said, "back on the rocks." He held out Quentin's sodden body. I lifted him into my arms and pulled my coat around him. His head hung from his lifeless neck, his legs dangled limply down, and his body was freezing and wet. I could not feel his heart.

"I'm sorry," said Tom as he clambered off the Judge and joined me on the step. "It was the journey back what did him in-that sea... oh, it was bitter. When I found him, "He said to tell you that he'd seen 'm."

"Thank you," I answered blankly. "I have your shirt

here and the Judge's hat and robe."

The Judge slowly eased himself from the water and stood looking down with his black, swimming eyes. "I'm very sorry," he said slowly. "No one expected it to end this way. He was weak when we found him but simply beyond happy to think he would be going home. And now you can take him there. Wrap him up in my old smoking jacket-that's the thing to do."

"Thank you," I replied weakly. "He would like that."

I carefully laid his body on the soft velvet lining and arranged his head so that he appeared to be sleeping, then folded the robe around him, creating a parcel that I tied together with the cord belt.

I was about to lift it into my arms when Robin hopped out of my pocket.

"Where is he?!" he asked. "Is he in there? I can't believe that he's asleep already-I bet he must be cold! Maybe if I snuggle up next to his chest, I can warm him up." And without waiting for a reply, he squeezed into the folds of the robe. "I found him," I heard his muffled voice say. "My, he IS cold, but I'm sure he'll warm up soon. Can you take us home now, please?"

"But Robin, you don't understand," I said, "you couldn't possibly stay there." I felt sick "Let them be together," whispered the Judge. "It's the right thing to do."

"Is it?" I asked, and I sat on the step with the cold wind blowing, and I wept.

"Take them home," he said kindly, resting his large, warm flipper on my shoulder. "There is no comfort for you here."

I got to my feet and clutched the precious package to my heart. There was a little opening at the top, and I thought I could hear Robin chatting softly to his friend.

The Judge heard it, too, and smiled. "He's a lovely little fellow," he said. "Now, you'd better get going before it's dark. There's a trail up that way," and he gestured over past the ledge. "When you reach the top, turn right and follow the path. It travels along the edge of the cliffs-there's no room for error, so be careful. If you go this minute, I'm pretty sure you can reach the Old Bear's cabin before dark. He's not the most welcoming of characters, I'll admit-a bit gruff and ruff around the edges-but he won't hurt you. He'll have a good fire going, food, and somewhere to sleep. He's not used to company, but tell him I sent you, and he'll try to be cordial."

"Thank you," I replied blankly. "Thank you both."

"In the summer, we'll visit," said the Judge. "It's a long climb up those steps, but I've got my sense of adventure back, and young Robin can show me the library."

"I could never have got my dear friend back without you," I replied, "and you're welcome to visit any time. I suppose I should go now. Thank you so much for your help."

I leaned into the Judge, and he gave me a hug. His slick fur was still damp from the sea but surprisingly warm, and when I looked up at his face, his kind, sad eyes were glassy with tears.

"Goodbye, and take care of yourself and Robin," he said.

I looked down at Tom, who stood beside him. "Thank you, with all my heart-thank you," I said.

"'Twas no problem at all," he replied. "I was glad to have met him and helped him off that rock. He was a grand fellow, he was. It's a shame, such a shame."

He reached up his little hand, and I took it in mine. "It brings me comfort to know that he spent his last minutes with you," I said.

"You really should be going now," advised the Judge. "Every moment of light is precious-that path will be treacherous in the dark."

I turned and made my way toward the trail with my best friends in my arms and began my long journey home.

Chapter Nine

The Old Bear

The narrow, sandy path ran precariously close to the edge of the crumbling cliffs. It was dusk, and my shoulders began to ache from the weight of my friends in my arms. My heart felt heavy, and I couldn't think, as one step after the other, I made my way along.

At the top of the bluff, I looked out over the bay and spotted Rookscroft far off on the hill. It sat, tucked into the landscape, looking away from me, out to sea. A faint light shone from the bedroom window, a beacon guiding us home. I traced the line of the back of the hill and imagined that I could see the gate-next to it would be the rosebush. That would be the place to lay him to rest, and along the lane was the church for the service. I would fill it with flowers, roses if I could find them so early, and freesias; he loved the smell of the yellow ones the best. The thought made me cry, and I let the tears run down my face as I continued along the path.

Dusk settled over the landscape, but still, there was no sign of a bear. I heard an owl's haunting call-low and empty-echoed by others far away. Soon it would be night.

As darkness fell, my mind wandered into a blank grey realm of emptiness. My body took one step after the next-the right, the left, the right, the right...

...The ground had gone! My foot found nothing but air, and my heart leaped to my throat as I pitched backwards, falling on the rocky ledge. Pebbles skittered over the side, disappearing into the roaring sea below. The icy wind lashed at my face as I clawed my way back to the safety of the path.

My friends? I felt around wildly in the darkness until I touched the velvet robe with my fingers and pulled it to my heart.

Everything was black. The sea churned wildly as it crashed against the rocks. I sat, too scared to move, my heart thumping in my chest. The cold began to pick at my coat with its icy fingers. We couldn't stay here for the night; we would all freeze.

In the utter darkness, I began to pray. I prayed for help, for guidance, for the ability to see-and then the miraculous happened.

In the black night, a pinprick of light appeared, then another and another, and as I watched, they began to grow into glowing golden spheres, like candlelight without a flame. They hovered just above the ground, and I stared in disbelief as I tried to understand what was before me. More of them appeared, gently flickering into life-five, six, seven, ten-all hovering together. I felt the loving presence of them all, and a voice inside my mind said, "Follow and we will lead you home."

I got to my feet, cradling my dear friends in my arms, and gingerly stepped towards them. As I drew near, they began to slowly bob and sway, just inches from the ground. They drifted along the path, just a few steps ahead of me, leading us to safety.

I was mesmerised by their gentle ways. They seemed to be talking together, but I did not hear them speak. Two of them were larger, about the size of a dinner plate, and the others varied in size from a saucer to an egg. There was something about their golden radiance, something familiar and comforting.

I can't say how long I followed them through the dark night, but after some time, the smell of sweet woodsmoke reached my nose, and it brought my attention back to the trail. I saw firelight between the trees, and there, to the left, set back in a little clearing, was an old wooden cabin with a wide front porch under a sloping roof of rusty tin. In front of the cabin, a wood fire blazed, and a bulbous pot sat between the flames. From its top, a copper tube rose and twisted before curling to the ground next to a rocking chair. Sitting on the chair, I saw the great hulking figure of a bear.

If I had come upon this scene at any other time, I would have run, but my heart was empty, and my mind was done. Better to be eaten quickly than to go on, so I continued towards him.

The old bear lifted his great head toward the sky and sniffed with his wide black nose. "Who goes there?" he bellowed. "Be off! This is private land!"

I didn't even attempt to reply but continued forward until I entered the circle of the fire.

"Go away!" shouted the bear angrily. "There is nothing for you here!"

I stood before the flames and regarded him.

"I said be gone!" roared the bear. "You're not welcome here! Go now and leave me in peace!"

The Old Bear by His Fire

He leaned forward in his chair and slowly rose to his feet. "I don't have time for this," he roared as he grabbed a long stick and began to walk towards me, brandishing it in the air.

I observed the scene impartially from a little vantage point deep within my head. A bear was approaching; he was mad. These were my last moments, and I felt grateful in a way that it was over.

He towered over me, and I felt so small as I held my dear friends tightly in my arms. Then, bending down, he examined my face, moving his huge head from side to side as he assessed me with his small, shining eyes.

I felt a tear run down my cheek. He looked at my arms and sniffed the bundle, and his face softened.

"I suppose you'd better come in. Follow me," he mumbled, and I walked behind him to the cabin.

The main room was cosy. A sturdy sofa, built from logs and strewn with blankets, faced a crackling fire. At the far side was a kitchen with a great stone sink full of apples. Crates of bottles littered the floor.

The air smelt of beeswax, honey, and apple juice, and somewhere in my heart, a small glimmer of hope sparked to life.

"Go sit by the fire," instructed the bear, "and lay down your burden."

I carefully placed the robe near the hearth.

"It's not a burden," I said weakly. "These are my friends."

The bear watched carefully as I slowly untied the arms of the robe and began to peel back the layers until I lifted the last, revealing Quentin and Robin, and I began to cry.

Quentin lay on his side, his legs tucked up to his chest, toes curled. His neck was bent around his body as if he were asleep, and Robin lay under his wing, his little head resting on the yellow feathers.

In the flickering firelight, they both seemed alive.

"Here, take this and drink it down," commanded the bear, passing me a small cup of apple wine. "It will help warm you."

I tipped back the cup and felt the hot drink in my throat. It warmed my stomach and cast a soft haze over my mind. Then, sitting down beside my friends, I gently stroked the soft feathers on Quentin's neck. They were dry now and glowed orange in the firelight, with bands of black at the tips. I had always been so captivated by the brilliant spirit of my friend that I had never looked at the details of his feathers before.

My attention wandered to little Robin. He sighed, then raised his head and looked around sleepily.

"Are we home already?" he asked weakly. "My, that is a lovely fire! I don't suppose you had a chance to make a cake yet? Is Quentin still sleeping? He must be very hungry by now."

"Dear little Robin," I whispered, "I don't think Quentin is going to wake up."

"Oh, I'm sure he will! I know he's tired, but he would love a bite to eat. It's not nice sleeping when you're hungry; it gives you funny dreams."

"I think we might have lost him," I said.

"Oh no, we haven't. Look, he's still here," replied Robin, brushing his cheek against Quentin's side.

"I don't mean quite that way," I said. "Oh dear Robin, I think he might be dead."

"Dead?" cried Robin. "You mean not alive, like that chair? But I'm sure he's not made of wood. Are all dead things made of wood? Because trees are also made of wood when they are alive... Does that mean that the chair is made from a dead tree? That's sad. I like trees; they are always good to talk to."

"Everything dies," I answered. "Trees and bees and birds and people, flowers and grass and foxes and flies. We are here for just a short time, and then we move along."

"Move along? To where?" asked Robin.

"Well, that depends on who you are," replied the old bear, who had walked over from the kitchen with a tray of food.

"You see, little fellow, none of us really knows, but we forest creatures live in a world of nature and magic, and we see that all life is connected together. So wherever it is we go, we are never apart."

Robin sat up and looked over at his dearest friend, then stared into the fire deep in thought before finally turning back. "And just one last question, please," he asked, his little voice shaking.

"Of course, you can ask us anything you like," I whispered, and the old bear nodded.

"Does your heart still beat when you are dead? I only ask because Quentin's heart is beating. I can feel it with my cheek."

As soon as he spoke, I saw a change in Quentin's face as though a veil of life had been softly draped over it. The white, lifeless flesh around his eye flushed the palest pink as his chest rose and fell. As I watched in astonishment, his eyelids slowly parted, and the glassy yellow eyes I loved so dearly moved around in their sockets, taking in the room.

"Robin, is that you?" he asked in his dear scratchy voice.

"Yes," replied Robin almost matter-of-factly. "It's me. I'm glad you're awake again, Quentin. Only Jayne and the bear were just telling me about death and wood, and it's ever so interesting if you would like to listen."

"Old Bear?" asked Quentin, lifting his head weakly and looking around. "I didn't know we had visitors."

"I think what you need is some food and warm water," I suggested, trying very hard to sound casual, although inside, I was bursting with delight.

"Warm water, yuck! I'm not an invalid, though I wouldn't say no to a spot of tea," replied Quentin, attempting to rise. "Oh dear, it seems that part of me is not working."

I leaned over and propped him up on the robe. "I'm sure you're going to be fine," I said. "You just need warming up. You've been on quite the adventure, and I'm so happy you are back. Now rest back down, and I'll see about the tea."

Quentin lay back, took a deep breath, and half-closed his eyes.

"I don't have tea as you are used to it," said the bear, "but I can make him a cup of warm mulled apple juice."

"I think that will be lovely," I replied, "and he could do with something to eat if you have a little to spare."

"I'll bring some wild seed bread and honey on the tray," said the Old Bear. "It might be bland to your folks' taste, but it gets me by. And I have some dried blackberries-I'll chop 'em up fine for your friends. Now, if you'll excuse me, it's my time for a nip of brandy. Would you care to join me?"

"I would be delighted to," I replied. "Do you make it in your still?"

"I do," answered the bear, and without another word, he disappeared into the pantry, returning minutes later with a tray, which he set down on the hearth.

He handed me a small cup with a gruff "drink up" and what almost passed as a smile.

I did as he suggested, then soaked a little of the seed bread in the apple juice for Quentin while Robin began to peck happily away at the dried fruit.

"Are they still here?" asked Quentin while we waited for the bread to soften.

"They?" I said.

He looked around the room, his eyes seemed soft and dazed. "My family."

"It's just me, Jayne, and a big bear," replied Robin helpfully, "but it's not a big cabin, so I don't think there's room for many more-unless they're very small, that is."

"They were with us on the path, and I thought they came in," replied Quentin. "They brought me back here from the other place, but I don't see them anymore. But wait... Yes, they're up there, waving goodbye," and his eyes settled on the dimly lit corner of the ceiling near the door.

I turned to look. It was very dark, but I thought I saw a soft glow melt into the shadows.

"Take care," whispered Quentin. "I'll miss you till I see you again. Thank you for returning me to my friends." And he sat for several moments, looking up.

"Are you speaking to a spider by chance?" asked Robin curiously. "Only, I do like spiders-the small ones, anyway. The larger ones scare me a bit; I think it's all those legs... and eyes."

"It was my family," replied Quentin. "They were with us, Robin; they guided us here away from danger and I'm so happy I got to see them again. They went missing when I was just a chick, and I was told they had perished in a terrible disaster, and that's how I grew up thinking of them, with the sad, dark end playing over in my mind. It tainted my life with a sort of melancholy, always thinking of them that way. But now I know that ill-fated day was just a moment in their eternal journey and they are always close by, watching over us, and they are happy. And now I can be happy, too."

His face looked transcendent in the glowing firelight, and his eyes sparkled. "And now I'm back, and I can't wait to be home again. My, what a fine time we'll have at Rookscroft; I'll never leave its walls again... Is it far?"

"I'm afraid so," I replied softly. "We travelled around the island to get you from the sea, and now we are again at the edge of the Wild Woods, which we must cross on our journey back home. Let's not worry about that now. Eat a little, my friend, and then you must rest."

We all settled down by the fire. The brandy soothed my mind, and being back with Quentin and Robin filled my heart with such deep comfort and delight I couldn't stop smiling.

Quentin sipped his juice and nibbled at some crumbs of bread, and I watched as he and Robin whispered together, sharing food from the same plate. I wasn't sure where we were, but it felt like home.

"Come and sit up here with me," growled the bear, and he patted the seat beside him. "It's softer than the floor."

I pulled myself onto the vast sofa, and I curled my feet under me. I felt so safe and small. The danger had passed, and we were safe now. I pulled a blanket around my shoulders as the old bear stared into the flames, and that is the last thing I remember before slipping off to sleep.

The popping logs woke me. The bear stood by the fire, stoking it with an iron pole. My friends were sleeping on the robe, which had been gathered round to form a nest, and I watched as he paused tending to the fire and tenderly draped a velvet sleeve over Quentin's back.

I yawned, and he looked over. "Ah, you're awake again, I see," he rasped.

The Old Bear

"Yes," I replied. "Is it very late?"

"That all depends on who you ask," he said. "I stay up sometimes past dawn. Is there something I can get for you?"

"I'd like to get some fresh air," I replied. "Do you mind if I step out for a moment?"

"Not at all," said the bear. "It will be a fine view now that the clouds have blown over."

I pulled on my boots and coat and went onto the porch. The cold north wind had cleared the sky, revealing constellations in all their glory. To my right, a line of the sea gleamed in the moonlight, and to my left was a great dark mountain swathed in trees. The world looked fresh and glorious.

It was lovely to step back through the door into the warm and welcoming room. The old bear walked in from the kitchen. "Come, have another drink," he said, and without a word, I took the small cup from his paws, and we sat down together by the fire.

"It's been so long since I had company. Now tell me where you are from."

"We live in the Rookscroft house," I began. "I think you might be able to see it from your porch on a clear day. It's a long way on foot through the woods, but it's up on the hill on the other side of the bay."

"That old house," said the bear, laughing. "Yes, I know it well. We are connected in one way or another, that old house and I."

I waited for him to elaborate, but he took a drink of brandy, sighed. "And what brought you here to the forest?" he asked.

My heart skipped at the very thought of it-the dark trees, the narrow paths, how easily things could go wrong there, very wrong. And now we had to enter them again if we wanted to get home.

"It was a mistake," I said.

"So, you live in that house yonder?" asked the bear.

"Yes," I replied, "and my friends live there with me."

"And you want to get home? Well, I'm guessing you don't want to go back through the Wild Woods, especially from here where there is no path."

"I would do practically anything to avoid them," I replied.

"Well, you'll be glad to hear there's no need for you to

travel through them again," he said.

"Is there really a way?" I asked. "I know that it's not too far across the bay, but those cliffs-it's surely impossible to get down to the water, and then how could we possibly climb back up the other side?"

"Oh, there's a way," laughed the bear. "There's always a way, and I need a nip more brandy-would you care for a little?"

"No, no thank you," I said. "It would send me straight to sleep."

The bear nodded, filled his glass, and almost smiled.

"Well, that house and I go a long way back. It really depends on how far you'd like me to go," he said.

"You're welcome to start at the beginning," I replied. "We have all the time we could wish for."

"Very good," said the bear, with a twinkle in his eye. "If you will indulge me, I don't often have guests. I can't say I welcome them as a rule, but to have a captive audience is a rare treat, and I intend to savour it."

I curled up in the corner and pulled a blanket under my chin.

"That house, Rookscroft as you call it, was built by Fritzl Albrechtsberger a long time ago. They say he built it so elaborate and strange to remind him of his own home in Bavaria, and I'm glad he did-it cuts quite the figure up there on the hill. Officially, Fritzl made beer-oh, and it was good stuff, strong and with a unique taste like no other. And there was a secret to that.

"He found a spring, up next to the house, with fine clear water to make his brew,. In its heyday, there were endless lines of carts carrying crates of beer down to the harbour, where the tall ships took them all over the world. But what few knew was that he had a little side business in brandy. He planted a large orchard, you see, all around the house, and he pressed the apples in the stable block. They'd fill up barrels with the apple wine and send it down the staircase."

"The staircase?" I asked.

"Yes," replied the Old Bear. "There's a staircase that leads from the door at the back of the stables, all the way down through the rocks, and it pops out by the water's edge on the other side of the bay. Well, my great-grandfather built this cabin here and he would go over on the raft to pick up the barrels and bring them back. When the wine was ready, he would turn it into brandy, then put it back in the barrels and leave it to cure. When they were ready, he would put the brandy into bottles and send a call out for the Obscura."

"The Obscura?" I asked. "Was that a boat?"

"Not was, IS," replied the bear. "It's a boat and a half, it is too. A steam-powered schooner, with a smooth ride and a great crew. In the old days, they'd pull up at the dock below, pick up the brandy, and off they'd go to sell it. It was the best there ever was, and no mistake-favoured by rich and poor alike, and one hell of a medicine for anything that ails you."

"And you said there was a secret to the beer?" I asked.

"That's right," said the bear. "We'd get the apple wine for free, and when the brandy was put into bottles, we'd send those brandy barrels back over and up the stairs they'd go, to be used for the beer making. Now, Fritzl's beer was good as it was, but after a few months sitting in the barrels, it was something really special-that's how he made his fortune."

"Was that a still I saw over the fire?" I asked.

"Why yes," replied the Old Bear, "and the brandy you've been sipping-I make that too. Just for myself nowadays, but it's good to keep the old ways going."

"And where do you get your apples?" I asked.

"Well, my grandfather grew our own orchard from seeds," replied the bear. "It's behind the cabin, and it suffices." He paused and took a swig from his cup. "Now it's your turn for a story-tell me how you came to be here in the Wild Woods."

"Well, we found a picture of a lodge when we were in the library, and it had a map and a key, so we set out on a little trip to find it-but everything went wrong."

"That happens here," said the Old Bear. "There are all kinds of beasts in the woods that you and your friends are best not meeting-even I don't wish to meet them. It's a wonder you didn't come to a rum end."

"We almost did," I replied, "but we met so many lovely new friends there too, and without their help, we would never have found our way."

"That's good to know," replied the bear. "I don't suppose I know any of 'em. I tend to keep to myself."

"Well, you do know one," I said. "Judge D.P. Bonneville-he rescued Quentin from the sea, and he's the one who told me to find you."

"Oh, did he indeed?" chuckled the bear, his eyes shining. "Well, he's quite the old fellow, and no mistake. I haven't seen him in an age. You know, one of these days I'll pay him a visit and take him a bottle-he likes a snifter with his pipe."

"I'm sure he will love that," I said. "And when you go, can you please thank him again for us? Quentin would have died without him, and I can't even bear to think of that."

"I will," laughed the bear. "And now I think it's time for me to head to bed and for you to get a good sleep. It's a big day tomorrow, but don't worry-I'll get you all safely home."

I sighed and closed my eyes. My body felt heavy and tired, and I fell asleep before he had left the room.

Chapter Ten

The Staircase

In the morning, I was the first to wake. I rose from the sofa and checked on Quentin and Robin, who were sleeping wrapped together in the robe, and I quietly made my way across the room to the door and stepped outside.

The view from the porch was spectacular. The early morning sun was rising over the snowy mountain range that spanned the horizon, tinging the sea with its rose-golden rays. I could make out the rooflines of the cottages in the harbour, and tracing the line of the hill, I saw Rookscroft looking out to sea. Below, in the bay, the emerald water lapped against rocks as it churned with the tide.

"It's quite the sight isn't it," said the Bear. He was standing behind me, holding a steaming cup in his great paw. "Here, I've made you a breakfast brew. You will need it for today," he passed over the heavy cup, which I took from him with both hands.

"See, there's the entrance over there," he said, pointing down with a sharp black claw. Far below, where the rocks met the sea, was a plateau that led to an opening where a line of stone steps disappeared into the cliffside.

"How do we get there?" I asked. "Do you have a boat?"

"I have a ferry of sorts," replied the Bear. "It's a raft that I can pull across the water with a rope, but only on a slack tide. They used to use it for the barrels in the old days. I admit it's been a while since I've been on it, but I reckon it'll get us over."

"Is it very deep?" I asked, looking down at the clear green water, and I felt a twinge of fear at the thought of crossing it on an old raft.

The old Bear sensed my trepidation. "It will be fine," he said gruffly. "I will get you all home safely, even if I have to swim you over on my back. Now shall we go back inside? I think I hear your friends..."

The Staircase Home

Quentin lay on his side on their makeshift nest, and his head was raised as he looked around the room. Little Robin was trying to help him up without success.

I went over to them and lifted the sleeve of the robe from Quentin's back. He lay on his side, his legs tucked up and his toes tightly curled like the day before. "I can't seem to get my legs to cooperate," he said. "They're just kind of there, and I'm not sure I can feel them."

I carefully lifted him and took him to the sofa where I could take a closer look. They felt very cold to the touch, their bright yellow colour had faded to a creamy fawn, and the ends of his toes were blue which was very concerning.

"Maybe if I gently rub them, I can get the blood moving," I suggested.

"Please do," replied Robin, who had fluttered up next to us. "We need to get him better by this afternoon so we can dance together in the kitchen."

"I'll do my best," I replied. I rubbed my palms together until they were warm and carefully took his left leg in my hands. It felt cold and scaly. Quentin watched closely as I gently massaged it, and when I reached his foot, I cupped my hands around it and warmed it with my breath. His poor toes were like ice.

"I think I feel something," he said. "Yes, I really believe I do." Encouraged, I blew again and rubbed his toes one at a time, and little by little, the colour returned.

I repeated the same process with his right leg, but when I was done, I noticed that the left one looked the same as it did before I started and the colour had faded and the blue had come back.

I quickly tucked them in the blanket.

"Are they better yet?" asked Robin.

"I do feel the blood returning, but I still can't get them to work." replied Quentin.

The Bear came in from the kitchen with a tray. "I've got some good vittles that will set us up for the journey back," he said, and he set it down next to us. There was a large chunk of seed bread with honey and warm herbal tea. I poured some tea in a saucer and added the bread to soften it, then offered it to my friends, and together we ate.

"Will it take very long to get back?" asked Robin curiously.

"It shouldn't be too bad. You'll be home well before dark," replied the Bear. "As soon as we're over the water, it's just a matter of stairs."

"I can't feel my feet yet so I'm not sure about the stairs," said Quentin. "And what's this about water? Please tell me you don't mean the sea."

"Well, yes," replied the Bear. "The bay, at any rate. We have to cross it on a slack tide, so we need to leave soon. But don't worry, everything will be fine."

"He's done this so many times before, it's second nature," I assured them. "And the stairs on the other side will take us right up to the stables at home!"

"Really?" asked Robin. "Is it a secret passageway for pirates? I hope we don't meet them, but I wouldn't mind looking for their treasure."

"Pirates? No," laughed the Bear. "Though I admire your sense of adventure, my little friend. My great-grandfather and old Fritzl built the steps so they could, let's say, engage in trade."

"Well, that doesn't sound so exciting," replied Robin. "But perhaps pirates used it anyway-they were like that. I'll keep a lookout for anything shiny. I'd love to find a trinket to go in my box of special things. I have very sharp eyes, you know."

"I don't doubt it," replied the Bear with a smile. "Now, if you'll excuse me, I'd best get some supplies together. We're going to need oil for your lamp, and I think I have just the bag for Quentin's ride home." He shuffled off to a back room, leaving me alone with my friends.

"How do your feet feel?" I asked.

"They don't," replied Quentin bluntly.

"I'm sure they'll come back," I assured him. "Here, let me try warming them again..."

I unwrapped them from the blanket (they had not improved) and I gently rubbed his toes between my palms, he sighed and slowly lolled his head to one side till it lay on my lap.

"I think he's taking a nap," said Robin.

"He is," I whispered. "It's going to take a while for him to feel like his old self again, but bit by bit, he'll come around with our good care."

"I think a slice of cherry cake might be what he needs," suggested Robin. "It always cheers me up, and the sugar gives me energy."

"I'll see what I can do when we get home," I said.

The Bear returned with a can of kerosene and an old carpet bag with a leather shoulder strap.

"If you wrap him back up in the robe and pop him in, I think it will do the job," he suggested.

"It's perfect," I replied. "So like the one we lost in the forest."

"They were often like that in the old days" Said The Bear and he looked towards the door, "Well, not to sound pushy, but we need to get going if we're to beat the incoming tide. I'll fill your lamp while you get ready."

I lined the bag with the Judge's robe and carefully placed my sleeping friend inside, then folded the fabric around him to keep him warm.

"Can I pop in too?" asked Robin, and without waiting for a reply, he hopped right in and disappeared beneath the velvet folds.

I put on my coat and boots, tied my lamp to the rucksack which I hoisted to my back, and we were ready to go.

"I can carry them," said the Old Bear, and he lifted the carpet bag with ease. Together, we left the cabin and headed out.

The path down to the water was steep, but thankfully the steps were wide and shallow, and within twenty minutes we had reached the wooden dock.

At the far end, a battered raft made of old wood bobbed in the water. A rope strung across the bay ran along its middle, supported by a post with an iron loop at each end.

"How on earth did they get the rope all the way across?" I asked.

The Bear looked across to the far side of the bay. "I believe they used the Obscura to help them," he replied. "I haven't been over in the longest time, but I'm pretty sure it will hold."

This wasn't reassuring, but I silently followed him over to the raft and tried to hide my fear.

It looked decrepit up close, with holes that had been patched with odd planks of wood and a rusty piece of tin from the roof. The Bear stepped effortlessly across in one stride and lowered the carpet bag to the floor, then turned and held out his paw. "Grab on and skip over," he instructed.

Instinctively, I reached toward him, and was about to touch his palm when a wave rippled by and the raft rose up. My heart lurched as I glanced down between the raft and the dock at the deep, icy sea that separated them.

"Here, have another go," encouraged The Bear, and again I leaned forward and took his paw. I closed my eyes, took the largest stride I could, and felt him pull me onto the raft, which bobbed about on the choppy water. "Take a seat on the floor with your friends, and I'll pull us over," he said. I meekly did as I was told and held the carpet bag on my lap.

The Bear laid his huge paws on the rope and slowly began to pull us to the other side. From the water, the cliffs seemed to stretch up forever towards the sky. The raft rose and fell as the Bear rhythmically heaved on the old frayed rope. I looked up at his face and saw that his eyes were fixed on the steps that seemed so far away.

"We're almost in the middle now," he said without looking down, "and there's a current here that's pretty strong, so hang on-it's going to get choppy."

I wasn't sure what I was supposed to hang on to-there was nothing on the raft-so I curled around the carpet bag and closed my eyes. The raft groaned beneath us, bucking wildly as it rose and fell. I felt the pressure against the rope as the fierce current tried to drag us out to sea pulling at the raft until it began to tilt, and I gripped the bag until my fingers turned white and closed my eyes.

"We're almost over the worst of it," roared the Bear, and with one last heave, he pulled us over and the raft moved smoothly through the water towards our destination. I could see the end of the rope tied securely to a rusty iron ring embedded in the cliff face next to the steps-we were almost there, we were almost home.

When we reached the landing, the Bear hopped off with an easy stride and tied up his craft. I slowly got to my feet, and carrying the carpet bag, gingerly walked across the bobbing raft towards him. He took the bag from my arms and placed it on the ground, then leaned forward and helped me step across.

"Thank you for that," I said. "But I hope I never have to do it again."

The Bear began to laugh. "Try pulling it over," he said with a twinkle in his eye. "I'm not what I once was, that's for sure. I'm going to need more than one hot bath to get the knots out of my arms after this."

I looked into the mouth of the cavern where the stone steps led up into the darkness.

"I'm going to have to leave you now," said the Bear. "I have to get my raft back to the other side before the tide turns. I'll get your lamp lit-there's plenty of time for you to get up before the oil runs out. Now, there's a door at the top that opens into the barn, and next to it, you'll find the key on a hook."

"But what if it isn't there?" I asked. "What if we go all the way up there and I can't find the key, or the door won't open? I'll run out of light, and even if I could see, there's nowhere to go but back down here to this ledge and then what?"

"Don't fill your head with worries about what could be," replied the Bear. "Remember just keep going one step at a time, and everything will work out as it should."

Now I've got to be going-the wind's picking up."

I untied the lamp and he lifted the glass and lit the wick. The little flame burned brightly. "Here, take this," he said and he handed it to me along with an old flint lighter.

"Now you've nothing to worry about, you've got plenty of oil and if the flame were to go out, which it won't, you can light it again. I'll come and get it back from you one day, and maybe some apples too if you can spare them."

"Of course," I replied. "You're welcome to all the apples you could want. We have plenty to spare, and there is a limit to how many pies a person can eat in a year."

The Old Bear Heading Back

"Oh speaking of apples, here's a little gift for you" he said and handed me an earthenware bottle with a cork in the top. "Now I must get going, until next time..." He smiled and touched the brim of his hat. "You've got good friends" he quietly said "and friendship's more precious than gold. Take care of each other. I promise to visit you soon, and if you're lucky I'll bring you a bottle of brandy." His eyes sparkled in the morning light as he nodded a final goodbye then he turned, untied the raft, hopped aboard, and pushed off to sea.

I picked up the carpet bag and laid the wide strap over my shoulder.

"Are we home yet?" asked Robin from the bag. "Only it seems like we've been moving for a long time. I dreamed we were riding on an elephant-is that true? It felt very bumpy."

He popped his head over the lip of the bag and looked around. "Oh dear," he said, "this is not good, not good at all, we are very near the water in the mouth of a cave, sea monsters dwell in caves like this. I suggest we leave at once."

"We will," I replied, happy to have the company of my little friend. "We just have to climb these steps, and they will take us home."

"Oh, the pirate steps, yes!" cried Robin excitedly.

"Then I woke up just in time! As I mentioned before, I have a very keen eye for treasure, so I'll help keep watch. Where did the bear go?"

"He had to go home, back over the water," I said, "and when he gets to his cabin, he's going to take a nice hot bath."

"Ooh, I like that idea," replied Robin. "I think I would like one too, and Quentin could do with one too, he is a bit salty from all that sea."

"I'm sure we can arrange that," I laughed. "Now let's hurry along and climb back home."

The steps were wide and steep, and it wasn't long before my legs burned. Robin helpfully counted as I climbed, and he was past three hundred before I paused to take a break. We were in a narrow tunnel inside the hill that faded into pitch blackness at the edges of the lamplight. It would have been the stuff of nightmares if little Robin hadn't been there to keep me company. He never stopped counting and chatting, and thankfully never needed a reply, as I was quite out of breath and my arm ached from holding the lantern.

By the six-hundredth step, I was no longer looking ahead. My legs burned, and my lungs were aching, I kept my eyes on my feet willing them along.

"Oh look, a door!" said Robin. "There's a door in the wall, and I see a key too! I hope it fits the lock. Is this the end? I do hope so. I feel like I'm living the life of a mole, only not the nice Mole I stayed with, because his house was very comfortable. This would be a giant mole who liked going up and down alot."

Just a few steps ahead was the door, and to the left, on a hook-the key! Just as The Old Bear had said.

Once we had reached it, It took a moment to turn the lock, I felt a click, and the door slowly opened.

The dim light in the barn was unbearably bright after the darkness of the cave, and it took a moment for my eyes to adjust. We were standing in the very last stall of the stable block, where the circus ponies had been kept. Straw lay scattered on the cobbled floor, and a painted nosebag hung from the gate.

We were home at last.

Chapter Eleven

Home

I stepped outside the stables into a glorious spring day. It was almost noon, but the low sun was still behind the hill, and the ground was dotted with patches of lacy frost.

A robin, perched on the top branch of a bare elder tree, welcomed us home with his beautiful song, and I thanked him from my heart as I watched his chest glow orange against the ice-blue sky.

At the kitchen door was a basket filled with carrots, mushrooms, and small spring potatoes-a gift from Frank and resting on top, tucked between the vegetables, was a letter.

The Kitchen Door

The old brass handle, shiny from use, turned easily in my hand, and I pushed the green door open and stepped into the kitchen. The air was cool with the familiar smell of home. I placed the carpet bag next to the range and set about making a fire and once it got going. Robin, who had been resting on top of the robe, popped out his head and looked around.

"We're home," he said happily. "My, that was quick! It seems like only moments ago we were somewhere else, and now we're back in the kitchen like magic. I wonder how we did that."

"Yes, we're home," I laughed. "Thank you for keeping me company as we went up all those steps in the dark, I would have been very frightened without you. Would you like some tea? I'm thinking of making some griddle cakes to tide us over till dinner."

The robe began to move, and Quentin's sleepy head emerged from beneath a sleeve. "Did I hear mention of cake?" he asked weakly. "I might be able to pull myself together for a nip or two."

"Oh, Quentin!" cried Robin. "I'm very glad you're awake again. We had a wonderful adventure-Tt felt like we were riding on the back of a very bumpy elephant, and then we explored a pirate's cave where I kept Jayne company. But I didn't spot any treasure there, and now we're in the kitchen."

Quentin looked up at me quizzically, and I smiled. "I'm sure we all have stories to tell," I said. "Would you like me to lift you out of the bag and find you a comfortable spot?"

"I wouldn't mind you giving me a hand," replied Quentin, and then, to my amazement, he wriggled free of the robe and stood up.

"Quentin, your legs are working again!" cried Robin with delight. "That's such perfect timing because now we can dance together after dinner. I've been looking forward to that."

"One thing at a time," answered Quentin wearily. "I need sustenance first. Please lift me onto the sofa, Jayne, and tell me more about this cake."

I carefully placed him in a pile of cushions and draped a blanket on his back, then went to the pantry and found ingredients for the cakes.

"I was thinking griddle cakes to start," I said, "with currants and perhaps cherry jam and tea."

"Sounds perfect, do proceed." replied Quentin from the couch.

The batter came together easily in the bowl. I had made them so many times before. I found currants and a pot of jam, and before long, I was cooking them in an iron pan on the range.

Robin hopped onto the sofa next to his friend, who had settled on the cushions and was keenly watching as the batter cooked.

"I had a very big adventure," said Robin, "and I can't wait to tell you all about it. But I think perhaps we should eat first because my tummy is very empty, and I'm running out of the energy of life."

"The first batch is done," I said, as I slid a golden cake onto a plate, topped it with jam, and broke it into little pieces so it was easy for my friends to eat.

I made fresh tea, brought over the tray, and we ate together without a word. The kitchen was warming nicely, and just as we were done, the clock in the hallway chimed three. I put down my cup and drifted to sleep.

I woke up with a happy heart, knowing that I was home. The weak afternoon sun cast a glowing square onto the cupboard on the far wall. I took off my coat, hung it on the peg by the door, and put on my slippers. My friends were sleeping soundly and I began to think of dinner-a nice pot of hearty soup made with the vegetables that Frank had left would do the trick. I took the letter from the top of the basket. The envelope was small, and addressed with an elegant, flowing hand. A line of beautiful stamps decorated the top edge, and it was sealed with a dot of red wax on the back. I placed it on the kitchen table and went to peel the carrots at the sink.

"Is that a letter for us?" asked Robin. He fluttered over and looked it over. "Oh, it says it's for the friends! I can't wait to see inside."

"Neither can I," I replied, "and I think there was a little something in my pocket that's just for you, from the Mole family."

"Oh yes!" cried Robin. "Can you get that for me, please? Only, I think you might need it."

I took it from the pocket of my coat pocket that was hanging on a peg by the door and laid it on the table.

"If you wouldn't mind opening it, please, because my beak isn't very strong," he said, and I carefully untied the knot in the string and unwrapped the muslin to find a large black truffle.

"Oh, that's lovely, Robin! I can't believe you found it!" I gasped. "Would you like me to put some in the soup, or would you rather keep it just how it is?"

"Oh, let's put some in the soup, please!" Robin cried excitedly. "Only, Quentin will be so thrilled when he eats it. Remember in the beginning, before this all happened? That was his dream, and he's going to be so pleased that it got to come true."

I roasted the vegetables in an old iron pot-mushrooms, shallots, garlic, potatoes, and a stick of celery from the larder. Robin and I sat together on the sofa and dozed until the sweet aroma filled the room, and I removed it from the oven. I added salt and a hearty vegetable broth, then pressed it through a sieve and made a creamy soup. Robin watched as I shaved the truffle and added it to the pot. It smelled heavenly.

There was a flutter of feathers, as Quentin rose from his cushions and shook himself out. "Is that what I think it is?" he asked.

"Why, yes, of course!" cried little Robin. "I brought you home the king of fungi, Quentin! A real black truffle from the Wild Woods just for you, and Jayne has made it into a delicious soup, which we can now share together because that was your dream."

"Shall I lay the table?" I asked, "and we can have a real celebration meal together!"

"Oh yes, please," answered Robin.

"That truffle needs to be entertained like the royalty it is," added Quentin, and his yellow eyes glowed.

I laid the table with my best linen tablecloth and china bowls from the cabinet, where I also found a crystal saucer, which I filled with the cloudy apple juice the Old Bear had given to us. I found some wholemeal crackers in a tin to sprinkle on the soup, a tin of candied fruits left over from Christmas, and two beeswax candles I had been saving for a special occasion. The finest table I could manage, in honour of the truffle, who was given the finest seat on a silver saucer between the candles.

I placed a cushion on the table and brought over Quentin, whose legs were still too weak to walk. Robin sat beside him and we settled down to eat.

"It feels like Christmas," said Robin approvingly as I broke up the crackers and sprinkled them on the soup.

"Better than Christmas!" added Quentin as he eyed the truffle. "There's enough there to last the year. Where on earth did you find such a specimen?"

I placed the bowl of soup between them as Robin began to speak.

"Well, it's a long story, Quentin, and I'm happy to tell it if you would like to listen."

"I'd love to," replied Quentin, "but shouldn't you eat first?"

"Oh, please let me tell you while you eat," begged Robin. "I don't mind if my soup gets cold, but things don't feel real till I've told you about them. That way, when we're old, we'll share the same memories."

"Then by all means, go ahead," said Quentin, and he took a bite of the soup-soaked cracker. "Well, it's absolutely delicious," he exclaimed. "Really quite something! I never thought a common ground bird like myself would get a chance to taste such epicurean delights. Why, the truffle adds a wonderful earthiness, and... I need a second sip."

"Well, I did and I didn't find it really," began Robin. "Only when I woke up and you and Jayne were still sleeping, I couldn't wait to go and look for a truffle because I wanted to make your dream come true. I thought it would be a wonderful surprise if you opened your eyes and found one by your beak. So, I hopped out of the window and started my search. I scratched everywhere where one might be hiding, just under the soil. I think that's where they grow, but I couldn't find even the smallest one. Eventually, I got to the bridge, and I didn't think it was safe to go any further, but I was a bit thirsty by then, so I thought I would pop down the side to the stream and wet my beak.

"I was standing by the edge-it's very muddy there-when a very nice squirrel on a little boat came by. He was punting it along with a stick, and he came towards me and said good morning. He was very friendly, you would have liked him, Quentin, he had a lovely tail, and we got chatting. Then I mentioned truffles, and he said he had a few and he was happy to spare one. I was very excited, and then he invited me onto his boat because he was on his way up to the larder."

"And you just went with him?" gasped Quentin. "Surely you know not to trust strangers?"

"But he wasn't strange at all," replied Robin brightly. "He was ever so nice-squirrels are, aren't they? Did I mention his tail? He took me under the bridge and into the big pool where the waterfall drops in, and he tied up his boat in some reeds and helped me off because it was a bit tippy. The larder was wonderful, Quentin, just like you talked about-a little cave in the rock behind where the falls come down. There's a path that goes behind the water, and then you're there. I wish you could have seen it, but then the truffle wouldn't have been a surprise.

"All the little creatures keep their winter provisions there-lots of nuts and roots and bulbs and such. The squirrel took a sack of hazelnuts for himself and picked out this nice truffle for me, and he wrapped it up safely. Then we went back to his boat. He helped me get on board, but then he decided that he needed to go back and get a few pignuts for his dinner. I was by myself waiting, and that's when the heron came down."

"A heron?" cried Quentin. "Those beasts have swords for a beak, Robin. This is why you shouldn't be out alone."

"Don't worry, Quentin, he didn't eat me or I wouldn't be here," said Robin brightly. "But he was very big, and I think he was trying to stalk me in the reeds, so I untied the boat and pushed off with the pole, and it drifted off down the stream and under the bridge."

"And the heron?" asked Quentin.

"He flew off into the air, and I didn't see him again," replied Robin.

"I wonder if it was the same beast that we saw by the dam," hissed Quentin, and he shivered at the thought.

"It could have been," I replied. "Let's not think of it again."

"Well, the current took me off along the stream, and that's when I saw you both walking on the path. I called out, but I don't think you heard me. I saw you looking at the mud, Quentin-I thought you were looking for truffles-and then I just kept going. It was so fast that you went out of view, and then I started to feel a bit scared. I went past another bridge made of logs and then through some marshland, and then I was in the forest, and it was very scary and dark. The banks of the stream were very steep and muddy, and there were disconcerting noises, and a big owl was watching me from a tree.

"I thought that if I kept on going like that, I might fall off the end of the world, and that scared me the most because on the maps that's definitely where the most sea monsters live. And there are even sea serpents, which are like snakes but bigger, and they eat galleons. Then I was crying, and the water in my eyes made it so that I couldn't see properly, and then there was a bend, and the boat got caught in some tree roots, and that's when I heard the voices."

"Voices?" asked Quentin. "I'm almost too afraid to ask."

"Yes, the voices of Mr and Mrs Mole, though technically Mrs Mole is a vole, which is a bit confusing. You've met them, Jayne-they were ever so nice to me, and they gave me some cake to share with you, Quentin, but I'm sorry to say that I ate it all."

"Oh, don't worry about that. I'm just glad no one ate you," replied Quentin kindly. "Now do go on."

"Well, they took me back to their home on the riverbank, and I stayed there for a few days until Jayne came to collect me. Then we came and got you, and now we're home." His story done, Robin tucked into his food hungrily.

"Quentin thought he heard you call his name," I said. "But we couldn't see you, and we ended up travelling all through the Wild Woods to find out where you were."

"I did see you," said Quentin, "but not at the river. I saw you later when I was on that rock out to sea. I heard you say my name, Robin, and when I looked up, I saw two twinkling stars quite low, and I knew it was you both, watching over me."

"That's right," replied Robin matter-of-factly. "Yes, it was us, Quentin. Sacha was there too, but you haven't met him yet and you wouldn't have seen him because he's the colour of night. I didn't know that I could be a wandering star, but I like that idea very much. Tell me, was I very small?"

"The smallest and brightest of them all," replied Quentin softly. "I think it's time to go to bed. Would you like to ride up on my back? I think my legs can carry us both up the wooden hills."

"I would love that, Quentin, but I haven't trimmed my nails in days, and I think they might be a bit on the scratchy side."

"Oh, don't worry about that for now," Quentin replied, and I saw that his yellow eyes were misty. "It's a dream come true to be home with you both-I couldn't ask for more. Come hop on, and we'll go up together."

I opened the door into the hallway and watched as Quentin made his shaky way up the stairs, then returned to the kitchen and tidied everything away. I savoured the simple pleasure of being home again, and when I finally went up to my room, I found my friends at the foot of the bed, tucked into a blanket, sleeping peacefully together.

The following morning, I woke to another bright spring day. It was chilly in the house, so I hurried through the hall into the kitchen, which was still warm. I stoked the fire and made a quick bread with cherries and a pot of fresh tea to take up to my friends. I was just about to leave when I noticed the letter from the day before on the kitchen table, so I popped it on the tray and went upstairs.

Quentin and Robin were on the windowsill between the parted curtains, looking out at the view. I placed the tray on the bed and went over to join them.

"It would be over there," said Robin, "if only the ivy wasn't in the way, we might be able to see it."

"What are you looking for?" I asked.

"The Old Bear's cabin," replied Robin. "Only I think you could see this house from there, so you should be able to see that house from here."

"Perhaps," I agreed, "but you're right-there is a lot of

ivy on the wall out there. Here, let me open the curtains and we might be able to get our bearings."

The spring sunshine lit the hillside that ran down towards the shimmering sea, and sweet birdsong filled the air. I sighed as we stood together, looking out at the glorious view.

"It would be down there," said Quentin, "but the trees are in the way, so we can't see it from this window."

"Maybe later we can go to the attic," I suggested. "There are so many treasures up there and lots of odd little windows in the eaves-I'm sure we can see for miles."

"Oh yes, let's!" cried Robin. "You know how I love treasure hunting."

"Well, first, let's have breakfast," I suggested. "I made you some cherry bread."

We sat on the bed and ate together.

"Do you know if any pirates lived here?" asked Robin after he had finished the last crumb. "Only if they did, there really might be precious jewels in the attic."

"And what would you do with precious jewels?" Quentin inquired curiously.

"Well, I'm not sure," Robin replied, "but it would be fun to find them; then I might be famous, and I might find my name in a book in the library someday."

"I highly doubt we will ever make it into a book," said Quentin. "I don't mean to be a killjoy, but the lives of birds aren't generally of much interest to bookmakers."

"Well, maybe not a book then," replied Robin, who seemed quite unperturbed, "but possibly a little mention in the newspaper perhaps, if we find the pirate treasure, that is."

"I'm looking forward to having a good poke around in the attic, but I believe this house was owned by a beer maker from Bavaria, so I'm not sure about finding treasure," said Quentin.

"But it is very near the sea," Robin replied hopefully as he looked towards the window, "and, well, you never know..."

The room fell silent for a moment, and I listened to the gentle cooing of morning doves as they worked on their nest in the ivy.

"Say, shall we open the letter now?" Suggested Quentin.

"Oh yes, can we please!" Robin chirped in.

As I leaned forward to pass it over to them, and held it in my hand, I read the postmark for the first time which made me smile. I poured another cup of tea and settled back on the cushions to watch my friends as they huddled over the letter and began to read. Their eyes lit up as they darted from line to line down the page, and when they reached the very last word, they looked both up excitedly.

"It's an invitation!" Cried, Quentin.

"Please, can we?" asked Robin.

"Of course," I replied.

And that is how our next adventure began.

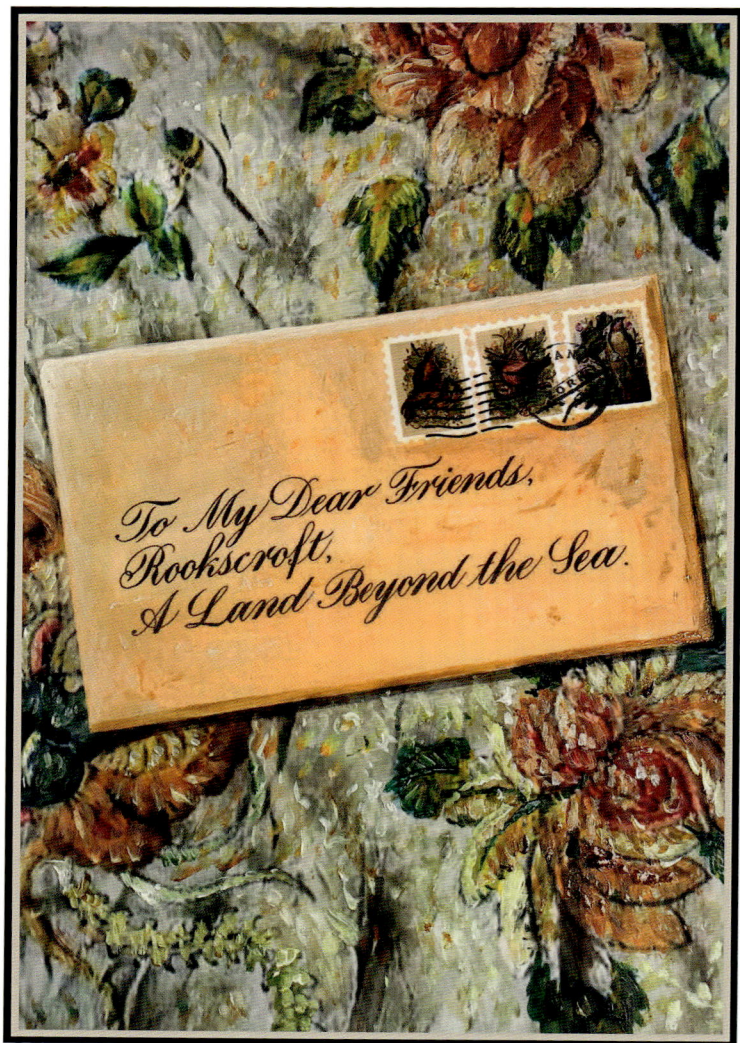

To My Dear Friends,
Rookscroft,
A Land Beyond the Sea.

A Letter From a Friend

Breakfast on the Bed

About the Author

Jayne Siroshton is an artist and author of whimsical, cozy fiction inspired by nature, folklore, and the quiet magic of everyday life. When she isn't writing or illustrating, she can often be found tending her garden, sipping tea, or spending time with her beloved animal companions.

She lives in a small village in Yorkshire, where she continues to create stories that invite readers into gentle, enchanting worlds.

Visit us at Rookscroft & Company in York, England or online at rookscroft.com for more books, gifts and exclusive content.